D. M. Greenwood has worked for twelve years in the Diocese of Rochester as an ecclesiastical civil servant, most recently as an advisor for Church Schools. Her first degree was in Classics at Oxford and as a mature student she took a second degree in Theology at London University. She has also taught at a number of schools and colleges of education. She lives overlooking the River Thames in Greenwich, London, with her lurcher bitch.

Holy Terrors

D. M. Greenwood

HEADLINE

ISBN 0 7472 4496 0

Printed and bound in Great Britain by
Cox & Wyman Ltd, Reading, Berks

HEADLINE BOOK PUBLISHING
A division of Hodder Headline PLC
338 Euston Road
London NW1 3BH

For Gwen and Marge Francis

Contents

CHAPTER ONE

St Veep's Girls' School

Members of St Veep's Girls' School began to arrive, in their different ways, about eight a.m. A chauffeur-driven Mercedes, the tinted glass of its windows rather thicker than normal, slowed down. Before it had quite stopped a nice mite of fourteen years hopped out and raced down the narrow passage between the senior and junior houses to the pupils' entrance. Minutes later the second mistress swerved into the gravel carriage sweep of the main entrance in a thirty-year-old grey Riley upholstered in real leather; many of its parts were original and those that weren't had been skilfully engineered by a garage mechanic at Miss Aldriche's rural weekend retreat. Ieuan Colt, second in the music department, freewheeled in on a powerful-looking motorbike. It had run out of petrol at the end of the square, but its impetus carried him easily into the staff car park on the opposite side to the pupils' entrance. Miss Barbara Brighouse would have preferred to have come in by horse but, failing that, strode in as though she had just got down from one, whilst Mrs Gulland

1

indicated her resentment at her newly divorced status (alimony settlement still in the hands of the lawyers) by tottering on high heels from the bus stop. She was forced to pick her way through a group of young Jewish girls of various heights emerging from a Volvo estate driven by a beautifully accoutred mother whose turn it was this Monday morning to convey seven equally smart Veepians from roads bordering the Finchley to the environs of Kensington. Three mathematicians arrived one after the other in rapid succession, dropped by solid-looking young husbands bound for the City, the Treasury and the *Financial Times*. The school, male and female – but mostly female – was gathering.

In the staff cloakroom, a basement immediately below the staff common room, the Pole who taught German greeted the Russian who taught French by flinging her arms round her shoulders and embracing her on both cheeks. With more restraint, after a separation of merely forty-eight hours, the Swiss who taught Italian, greeted the Argentinian who taught Spanish by shaking her warmly by the hand. The head of classics, Doris King, cringed with an embarrassment which ten years of witnessing such scenes had not diminished, and bolted up the iron staircase to the common room lest she too should be assaulted.

In the common room, Janet John smelt the scent which Oenone Troutbeck was wearing as she stood next to her glaring at the noticeboard, and deplored it. She moved downwind. She'd played cricket for England's Ladies and thought anything more exotic than the smell of leather and dubbin a betrayal of decent values. Secretly, and indeed without fully acknowledging it to herself, she found

Oenone attractive as well as intimidating: she particularly admired the way her colleague had of raising the right eyebrow without raising the left.

The notice at which they were both gazing read:

ST VEEP'S GIRLS' SCHOOL
75, STRACHAN SQUARE
LONDON W4

The Upper School Lent Concert of Sacred Music will take place on Thursday 17 April at 7.45 p.m. Invitations to parents and governors will go out by the end of seventh week. Heads of year please organise. The Senior School Orchestra will have the honour to be conducted by Sir Solomon Piatigorsky, the distinguished conductor. Staff will need to excuse girls from lessons for rehearsals from third week onwards. Mr Colt will arrange rehearsal times. Miss Brighouse will co-ordinate. I know the occasion will be a memorable one for us all. A.M.P.

'I wish she wouldn't tell us how distinguished everyone is,' said Miss Troutbeck. A tall woman, she stood behind her colleagues and eyed the notice from a distance. 'And if you were in any doubt about the function of conductors, they conduct.'

'Piatigorsky's tempi at *Aida* last night were eccentric', said Miss Brighouse, whose interests were wide. She was on her way to gather books and gave it but a passing glance.

'I hope he's not going to be too ambitious with our girls' tempi,' said Mrs Gulland, who never liked to be left behind in any conversation which combined social with intellectual snobbery.

'How does she know the occasion will be memorable

before it's happened?' said Mr Colt in his Welsh innocence, pausing in his effort to move his cello towards the door.

'Ah, the great Piatigorsky,' murmured the Russian who taught French.

'Can one use "co-ordinate" as an intransitive?' Miss King inquired to no one in particular as the gong sounded for 9.15 a.m. school.

Dante Gabriel Cromwell, head of art, who was on principle late for all engagements, did not spare the notice so much as a glance as he strode through the staffroom to collect his mail.

Having, as it were, cut their teeth on the first mistress's bone, they scattered in search of hymn books and Bibles, registers and markbooks, the paraphernalia of ordinary academic life, without which even St Veep's could hardly function.

The Reverend Theodora Braithwaite, a woman aged about thirty, and in deacons' orders in the church of England, peddled with easy sweeping strokes round the one-way system of Strachan Square, proceeding slowly enough to enjoy each side of the square in turn. Its north and south ends were made up of substantial brown brick villas hung about with bare lilacs and laburnums. At the west end of the square was a church, known at the turn of the century for the strength of its evangelical fervour and the menace of its apocalyptic sermons. Prebendary Webb-Peploe had been a frequent and popular visiting preacher, but now the splendid neoclassical façade proclaimed its new ownership by Greek Orthodoxy. Church of the Resurrection, it said in gold letters and Greek characters, on a red board. Theodora nodded to it as to a friend. She rounded the north side, freewheeled slightly downhill to the east side, then swerved into the carriage sweep of St Veep's. The school's chunkier façade in domestic Italianate glittered white and spruce in the thin April sunlight. She leaned her bicycle against the foot of the steps and mounted to the grey painted double doors.

St Veep's still took seriously its high calling to be a place of learning for women. Its past was a famous and honourable one. The detritus of its first pupils' early struggles could be seen displayed in substantial glass cases in the library. Greek texts showed careful annotations in ample margins written in the spiky script of women in the 1880s who only lately had been allowed to go where their brothers had gone. Their dictionaries and lexicons, second-hand when acquired from those same brothers, were lovingly repaired and bound. The Strachan Bequest. The Braithwaite Bequest. Photographs in yearly more fading sepia showed groups of young women holding, like an honourable company of pikemen, lacrosse sticks. Dignified in long skirts, boaters and immensely large ties flattened on rising bosoms, they bravely faced the unfamiliar camera.

The school's buildings were worthy of the solid aspirations of its founders. The large, marble-floored entrance hall, the heavy mahogany doors, the waxed oak panelling in every room, the figured glass and polished brass fittings subdued even those few who entered the school not intending to be impressed. Strong materials of the best quality put together to last at a time when labour was cheap and craftsmanship normal had worn well through the century. There were no foxed edges, no scratches on the panelling or smudges on the daily cleaned brass.

The financial arrangements of the founding ladies had been as sound as their architecture. St Veep's investments had prospered. The endowment, in the hands of prudent fathers and astute liverymen, had expanded decade by decade. Excellent quality they had sought – and mostly got. Early thrifty provisions had afforded the school wealth; even, in due course, grandeur. Those outside the circle were occasionally provoked to envy.

If they had inclined to see their daughters' education in terms of an investment, the founding fathers had always perceived that that investment must not be in anything ephemeral. Tradition, and piety towards that tradition, had in the school's early days married worldly success to classical and Christian values of truthfulness and public service. The established Church had quickly been drawn in. Two canons and a bishop sat ex-officio on the governing body. The very site of the school had been donated by the Church. A chapel had been required as part of the original building. A chaplain had been allowed for in the endowment. In this way fathers who might have been suspicious of the unsettling effect of education on their daughters were reassured.

As the twentieth century had progressed, however, relations between the Church and the liverymen on the governing body had become strained. The last two first mistresses had not been appointed for their piety; a first in Greats followed by a senior wrangler had seen to the academic quality of the institution rather than its religious ethos. What in the early days of the school had been a mere handful of young women progressing to Lady Margaret Hall and Girton had, by the retirement of the last head, become a flood of their granddaughters proceeding as of right to Balliol and Trinity, their place in the world as assured as their grandmothers but different, the scope for the exercise of both virtue and vice larger. At first the Church had concurred with the secular governors in taking a pride in the standards and achievements of the young females. Too late it had realised that, all unknowingly, its values had been usurped. Lip service was paid to Anglican teaching but no more than that.

The staff, originally drawn from the same ground as the pupils, had only recently begun to be recruited from a wider field. The first mistress-ship of St Veep's was a plum ripe for picking which had, a couple of years ago, fallen into its present holder's lap only after a great deal of manoeuvring on many parts, not least those of that holder. Dame Alicia Pound was, she prided herself, a very modern woman. The charming, self-deprecating smile disguised for some the heavy lantern jaw and immensely strong teeth. A career begun, after Cambridge, in journalism, had converted itself in its latter reaches into the upper echelons of the civil service. Secondments to various consultative jobs on quangos in Europe had added a patina of almost academic respectability, sufficient to secure a majority from the governors of the school at that crucial moment. They were looking for a more robust leadership and managerial style than had hitherto marked the office. As they thought. The more perceptive had held that the plain Scot who had steered the school through the seventies and eighties had shown more durable qualities: adroitness, a steely strength and a full-blown quiver of diplomatic strategies for dealing with all crises, financial or academic. Miss McGregor, however, had never for an instant flaunted these qualities. Dame Alicia on the other hand had never seen any reason not to show absolutely everything, preferably immediately on meeting for the first time. She made, it was said, a tremendous impact. Certainly she spoke very loudly and said everything twice.

'Dame Alicia wants a K.'

'I thought a D was the equivalent of a K for women.'

'Well, you know what I mean. The next one up.'

'Life peerage?'

'That's the one.'

'Why?'

'I suppose she has rather vulgar tastes. She's greedy and she's a woman of little imagination. I expect she can't think of anything else to grab.'

A pretty typical Veepian dialogue, thought Theodora, who had heard it as she strode from the front door across the marble-paved entrance hall toward the first mistress's rooms. The girls were not surreptitious, nor were they blatant, reaching for a sophistication that they did not possess. Any sophistication they had was their own and genuine. They were matter-of-fact, almost judicious in their manner. Their judgement was first hand, based upon a cool observation over two years. The twins Theodora had overheard would never themselves have dreamed of displaying ardour over anything. Jane and Josephine Hapgood sailed like swans towards the music room at the end of the corridor, serene in their excellent manners and identically competent intelligences. Theodora, whose own Cheltonian youth had also required the disguise of ardour, relished their accuracy.

She seated herself on the art nouveau oak bench opposite the first mistress's door. Her appointment was for ten-fifteen. The door had been disfigured on the advent of Dame Alicia by the addition of two lights: one red, which said 'engaged' and the other green. Dame Alicia had been dissuaded from inscribing 'vacant' on the green. The broad double staircase running off the hall wound up to the first floor. Theodora became aware of the murmur of young voices above her.

'Exeter will be full of hairy young men like Victor, in green

8

wellies and Barbours.' The voice was light, unemphatic.

'Ginny went there for an interview last term and she said she had quite a good session. The young man gave her sherry and was quite articulate about Boccaccio. She thought she might well accept, if the Courtauld won't have her.' The accent was slightly American.

'Music's poor, hunting's superb,' said the third in authoritative tones. 'My uncle's a canon of the cathedral,' it added.

'Just give me the ground rules again, could you?' said the American voice again. 'I'm allowed *either* Oxford *or* Cambridge but not both. And then four others, not necessarily in order of preference. Right?'

Theodora glanced upwards to the girls clustered round the life-sized replica of the Nike of Samothrace which presided in a distant sort of way over the broad landing at the top of the staircase. One of the girls was seated on the bench in front of it; one squatted on the floor beside her, her long black hair swinging forward over the UCCA form spread out in front of her, a bitten-looking pencil clamped between her teeth. The third, the fair-haired girl who had depreciated Exeter's males, stood a little to one side.

As Theodora looked up, the fair-haired girl looked down and caught Theodora's eye. The girl did not smile nor did she stare. But with complete self-possession she met and held Theodora's glance. With equal composure, in her own time, she withdrew her gaze and returned her attention to the group.

The light on Dame Alicia's door changed from red to green. Theodora gave it a count of three and then rose from the bench to her full height of six foot one and knocked.

Jessica Stephanopoulos, whose father was something at the Greek embassy, pushed her feet as far forward into her

9

indoor shoes as she could and then snapped each toe in turn against the leather. She did this when she was embarrassed. Scripture lessons embarrassed her dreadfully. Ten-thirty on Mondays was a low time. A heavy, solid day, you had to wade through a lot of facts on Mondays. People were being efficient. They walked about the school swiftly and purposefully, all being competent. Perhaps, thought Jessica dolefully, you had to start off efficient if you had the whole week to get through.

The young chaplain entrusted with teaching divinity, Jessica noticed, had a special vocabulary for his subject. 'Dwell', 'exalt', 'forsake', 'sojourn', dropped from his lips, words whose very sound were to Jessica's ear mournful. She supposed the Jews, about whom they appeared to be learning, were a special and mournful people. The Reverend Robert Mere's voice rose and swelled with the agonised rhetoric of his language as he got the 'children of Israel' way out into the desert. Jessica eyed the wiry young man with too little hair. His vowels, she realised, bilingual child of an international marriage, were rather genteel. He seemed well under way. He was pacing up and down across the platform, talking and talking in the peculiar, quasi-biblical language. Behind him, a meticulous copy of the *Light of the World* looked meaningfully out on to the neat rows of desks. On his other side, a sepia Moses in a night-shirt, his eyes rolled up like an Asiatic ecstatic, struck the rock in the desert. Christians and Jews were equally, if badly, served.

The curriculum at St Veep's was highly developed, constantly reviewed and appropriately revised. The exception was religious education. It was felt irreligious to subject it to the renovation that marked every other academic enterprise in the school. It lingered unscrutinised in a sepulchral Dark Age of Authorised Versions and maps of the Holy Land. The head of religious education had so far successfully fended off any forays on the part of the curriculum development committee to modify his intransigently boring and irrelevant syllabus. Apart from Rabbi Kassman who took Jewish prayers on Fridays, the Reverend Robert Mere taught the subject throughout the school on the minimum allotment of one thirty-five-minute period a week. If more souls were lost than saved by this regimen, Mere had come to feel that it was not his fault.

He had been attracted to the post of chaplain by the number of famous names which he recognised amongst the parent body. He'd not enjoyed his curacy in a parish in Hounslow, though his vicar had assured him he had a talent for preaching. So he had applied to St Veep's advertisement for a chaplain with a 'sound academic background'. Since his was the only application and the bishop had been insistent to his fellow governors that an appointment be made, he had got the job in spite of the misgivings of the senior staff. It took him very little time to realise that, with adolescent girls of the calibre found at St Veep's, he was not at ease. Indeed, if he were honest, he would have had to admit that he could scarcely cope. But he wouldn't resign; instead, he developed a series of evasions which more or less saw him through. By surrounding his subject with a powerful aura of holiness, he could stave off inquiry or intellectual debate which might put his own knowledge to the test. He discovered too that if he could infuse enough emotional intensity into even his most ordinary remarks, he could circumvent questions for which a degree in geography at Reading and two years at an evangelical theological college in the Midlands had not equipped him. He used no textbooks except the Bible and kept the critical independence of mind of his pupils at bay through sarcasm and deflation. With his colleagues on the staff he was jocular, facetious and knowing. The cloth, the collar, just about protected him from the contempt of women whom he patronised, and to whom he could not hold a candle.

Jessica fixed her eye with simulated interest on the Reverend Robert Mere and felt her way down the immense and comforting depth of her right-hand skirt pocket. Two toffees, her asthma inhaler, locker key and a dog lead gave place at the very bottom of her pocket to a solid metal object, round which her fingers curled. She jangled it between her thumb and two fingers, caressing the smooth cool metal and warming it into life. While her hand held it, she felt safe.

CHAPTER TWO

South-West London Comprehensive School

At seven-thirty on Monday morning, Mr McGrath wiped both hands down the front of his pale grey sweatshirt, thereby freeing them from the remains of his breakfast. He strapped on a leather belt of enormous girth – not, however, quite so enormous as his own girth – clipped two different sets of keys on to a chain hanging from it, and thus accoutred started out for work.

His caretaker's residence was some distance from his place of work. He lodged in the basement of a large Edwardian villa which backed on to the enormous plain which constituted the playing fields and immediate environment of the South-West London Secondary Comprehensive School in the parish of St Sylvester's Betterhouse.

It was a long haul across the steppe-like field. The April wind would have cowed a lesser man. But Mr McGrath did not flinch, nor did his pace vary as he approached the school's two tower blocks with their litter of hutted accommodation at their feet. They were like a couple of icebergs surrounded by seals, Mr McGrath thought, his years in the Royal Navy having given him an eye for such things. Up the north wall of the nearest block ran a web of scaffolding, now almost permanently in place to cope with the building's cracking decay as it entered the twentieth year of its existence. The site board advertised the diverse nature of the building industry in this part of London: Makepeace and Singh, Vouniki and Smith advertised their share in the economy of the area. At this hour the workmen could be seen in the site hut making their first brew of the day.

As McGrath neared the buildings, the steppe gave way to pure mud, lightly spiced with a litter of coke tins, broken glass and crisp packets. The composite stone paving of the path to the main entrance was fissured, and to left and right were signs of an intense and vigorously destructive life. Two raised beds of very tough hebes had alone survived from the ambitious planting scheme drawn up by the landscapers of the hopeful sixties. Mr McGrath's job description obliged him to take notice only of what was actually dangerous. The ugly or merely delapidated was not his concern. A skip full of broken plaster, and an immense coil of electrical cable, presaged the rewiring which was causing chaos within. He unlocked his way through pairs of plate-glass doors, sniffed the smell of commercial cleaner and coke fumes and dived down to his beloved boilers.

At eight-ten, three deputy heads – two male and one female though identically attired in denim – arrived clutching huge plastic holdalls. They slammed a variety of Japanese car doors and sprinted towards the main block entrance.

At eight-thirty a trickle of younger boys, skimpily clad in padded nylon jackets, began to kick bits of litter about at the edge of the mud, adding to it judiciously with offerings of the wrappings of breakfast snacks of Mars bars and crisps. Ten minutes later, older boys drifted in like a hesitant tide, as though unsure whether they would be staying, and began to divert themselves by tripping the smaller boys into the mud. Here and there a curl of cigarette smoke flared briefly before being caught by the wind. Pupils did not come by car or bicycle. They walked or else fell off buses as though released from a spring trap, all tangled up together. It was a neighbourhood school.

By eight-forty, two-thirds of the seventy-odd staff had begun to inhabit the factory-like structures. Striplights flickered on here and there in classrooms and laboratories. The smell of coke fumes increased. Girls of all ages but usually in gaggles of four or five took up their stances on the perimeter of the mud and began to jeer at the boys. By ten to nine most of those of the fifteen-hundred-strong pupil body who had decided to grace the establishment that Monday were milling around in the intense cold and beginning to move like marauding invaders towards the four pupil entrances of the two concrete blocks. At five to nine there was a rattle of keys and eight large P.E. staff members, two to each of the pupils' entrances, flung the doors open. With something close to a cheer, the horde of pupils began to pour inside.

Mr McGrath pulled off his boiler-house gloves, checked his keys and emerged from the infernal regions. He made his way up the main staircase of B-block, an uncarpeted concrete and steel structure, to the second floor. Unlike most of the junior staff, he did not need to fight his way through the unyielding scrum of pupils. His reputation was enough to secure him passage. Where a child was dilatory or unheeding, McGrath simply applied his ample hand to whatever part of the body was most accessible and swung him or her out of the way. He was much respected; he never used more force than was necessary. In this way he reached the staffroom.

He could hear the voice of the second deputy head at the far end of the staffroom as she ran her eye down her clipboard, and the plaintive tones of her colleague as he pleaded with her.

'I can't put more than fifteen in that rat hole.'

'I *know* you'll be a tiny bit squeezed, Ralph. But we've all got to make the best of it even if it *does* mean flying out the windows.'

'Thirty-eight B4 hasn't *got* any windows. That's my *point*. Apart from some noisy heating mechanisms, it hasn't got room for anything in it.'

'Well, you'll just have to think of it as a *challenge*. It's a marvellous opportunity for co-operative learning. Social . . . interactive . . . basic body skills . . . integrated . . . participative . . . learning situation.'

McGrath heard the incantation with interest.

'Yeah. A complete pupil-centred, project-based, autonomous learning slice of chaos. I am *not* taking a collection of thirty band seven fourth years, sorry, year tens, for drama in a room designed for fifteen to practise sitting still and breathing in.'

The deputy head never allowed herself to become 'stressed' as she would have put it. She had a degree in sociology from Ontario and was reading for a masters in the social psychology of micro institutions at London University Institute of Education, where she was highly regarded by her supervisors. The more agitated her colleagues got with her, the cooler, genuinely cooler, she found herself becoming. Tiny, with a cloud of dark hair,

she inhabited her dungarees beautifully. It made her difficult to argue with and it was a measure of his desperation
that Ralph even tried to.

She turned to McGrath as he hoved into view. 'Mike,
39B4 is still out of commission? Yes?'

'Yes.' He was going to say, 'Miss', because he'd spent
twenty-five years in the services and had an Irish father
behind him. But he prided himself on having picked up
the mores of the institution. 'First names in a rational
democracy of free equals. And that means all ancillary
staff,' the ridiculously young-looking headmaster had said.
So he replied, 'Yes, Cherry. It won't be ready before tomorrow. Not the rate they're doing it. It's the electrics takes
the time.' He refrained from adding that none of the electricians seemed to speak English and that would slow
things down, like as not.

Ralph, the ageing young man in cords (cords, McGrath
had learned, meant a member of the English department)
looked desperate.

'Cherry, love, you've got to find me something else. I
simply can't take ten seven in 38B4. It's got one of the
Kostases in it'. He clinched his argument with what he
clearly regarded as his trump card.

Miss Rumbold assumed a yet more reasonable air, if
that were possible. She put her small pretty finger to her
lower lip in a parody of thinking.

'There *is* the Councillor Ferrin Memorial Hall.'

'Yes,' said the desperate young man without hesitation.

'It's a *big space*, Ralph,' she said with concerned intimacy.
'You're sure your working parameters aren't going to be
unhandleable?'

'I'll keep the beggars in play. Thanks awfully, Cherry
love—'

His further remarks were drowned by a tannoy of incredible decibels cancelling all conversation. 'Good morning, everyone. May I have your attention, please?'

The headmaster, or headteacher as he preferred to be called, or better still, the senior management team leader, had swiftly acquired the nasal south London vowels which he felt appropriate to his situation and his carefully plotted advancement within the state education system. But just occasionally the imperfect reproduction of the sound system detected, like some prying archaeologist's trowel, the received pronunciation to which he'd been brought up. Subliminally Ralph noticed the stab of contempt that he always felt at being patronised by such a voice using such a medium.

'The staff absentee list for today is as follows. Miss Shepherd, Mr Singh, Mrs Godfrey, Ms Helliwell. So the room changes will be: Miss Shepherd's classes to Mr Troutbeck in 38B4, Mr Singh's classes . . .'

Ralph gave a yelp of dismay. 'I can't, I just *can't* cope with Muriel's lot as well as mine. It means I'll have the other Kostas boy.'

An hour later the Reverend Geoffrey Brighouse on a second-hand Lambretta bumped cautiously over the once decorative paving of the school drive, circumvented the roll of cable, and fell off in the general direction of the door. He was so numbed with cold he could scarcely see out of his eyes, so he almost cannoned into McGrath as he lurched through the glass door. McGrath had a respect for the cloth, even when it wasn't, by his Irish father's standards, proper, and he liked the gangling and energetic Geoffrey. He caught him adroitly with his left hand, much as he'd manhandled pupils on the staircase an hour before.

'A good way to get about in summer, sir. If you see what I mean.'

Geoffrey drew in deep breaths of the coke and cleaner mixture, which was at least warm, and turned his smile full on McGrath. 'Thanks very much. I can never decide whether it's better to go fast and get very cold but get it over with, or to go slowly and prolong the agony but not quite as much cold air rushing past.'

'It's a problem, sir. Myself I find it's best to take your mind forward to what you're going to do next so you don't notice too much.'

Geoffrey thought this sound pastoral advice, and said so. He unlaced his gauntlets and attempted to unbuckle his helmet, which made him look like an old-fashioned deep-sea diver, stamping his feet a couple of times to get them used to where they were in relation to the floor. He glanced in the direction of the empty guichet which said: 'All Visitors Report Here. No Pupils Before 11.30.' From behind the glass shutter came the clatter of typewriters. Deciding against announcing his presence, he mounted the stairs, now mercifully empty, to the staffroom.

Geoffrey opened the door cautiously and edged inside. The staffroom resembled a wide corridor. Along one long side were windows, along the other noticeboards. There were double doors at either end on the short sides. The view was of the playing field wastes. The familiar décor met his eye. It was not unlike an airport lounge at the height of an air-controllers' strike. Unwashed mugs of half-drunk coffee and overflowing ashtrays crowded the low tables. Unseated armchairs were piled with battered-looking exercise books. Luggage in knapsacks or plastic holdalls was prudently stacked out of the main flight paths against the walls. The low chairs and low tables had the effect of bringing the scale down to the horizontal, an impression reinforced by the semi-recumbent posture of a number of staff, apparently in the last stages of fatigue, spreadeagled *on*, rather than *in*, the untrustworthy chairs.

Geoffrey recalled the words of one probationary teacher, now long gone. 'South-West London Secondary is like a waiting room', she'd said. 'Half of the staff have just come and the other half are poised to move on.' It was true. Nobody loved it. It had been devised, in the teeth of opposition from parents and staff (briefly united) from two secondary moderns and a technical high school, in response to planners' decisions in the late sixties. It had had the vicissitudes of such institutions. Funds from the Local Authority had flowed freely for a time and then dried up. Chairmen of Education Committees had come and gone, leaving their names but not their thrusting spirits on the building; the Councillor Ferrin Hall, the Isaacson science block. It had an air of waiting for the next reorganisation to hit it. The school secretary was the longest-serving member next to McGrath.

The immense noticeboards, stretching from head's notices, through those of the deputy head, heads of house and heads of year down to the Union's, displayed the web of the institution. At the very end of the series there was a space left empty, perhaps to allow some small token of individual creativity to insert itself into the heavy concrete paving of the hierarchy. Here someone had scrawled in blue chalk, 'Dreadlocks unlock dread.'

Humbly, for it was not his terrain, Geoffrey fumbled inside his jacket pocket and produced a neatly typed notice:

St Sylvester's Betterhouse
Wanted for boot sale

last Friday of Easter term:
helpers, programme-sellers.
Staff and students, all welcome.
If you can spare an hour,
please give your name as soon as possible to:
Rev. Geoffrey Brighouse, St Sylvester's Vicarage,
Old Road, Betterhouse.

He was struck by the unobtrusiveness of the notice. Perhaps a logo or a bit of red biro would improve the impact? Geoffrey fumbled in his pocket again.

'Reverend Brighouse to go to headteacher's room immediately. Mr Springer is free now.'

It was a woman's voice crackling over the tannoy. It managed to convey, in the manner of secretaries the world over, that an honour was being conferred by her boss's order. The tannoy crackled again and three pips sounded. Immediately there was an enormous roar. The third teaching period had ended and the school had been loosed for break.

Geoffrey braced himself for the battle. He struggled through a mass of bodies, braving double doors swung in his face from expert, inimical hands. Boys cannoned off each other. Girls in all sizes but all redoubtable, many eating, their arms linked together, presented phalanxes more impenetrable than Alexander's army. Geoffrey made no judgements. He simply remarked the differences in physical conduct from his own school days. He had to admit that Rugby and Magdalen College, Oxford had not really equipped him in some respects for life at SWL. The navy's training in unarmed combat had been rather more useful.

He had to concentrate to find his way. Every corridor of

the four floors looked like every other corridor. All had windows on one side with the dire view of the playing fields and identical classrooms opening off the other side. Here and there graffiti showed through the thin cover of white emulsion on the walls. Geoffrey always liked the Arabic ones with their vigorous, elegant script; such a testimony to the efficiency of the Islamic community's Saturday schools, he felt.

The going was made yet more treacherous for pedestrians by the piles of nylon bags left in heaps outside the doors of the classrooms. No one trusted the lockers in the basement cloakrooms, their locks long since vandalised, their doors unhinged. So pupils carried round with them everything they needed for the day: games kit, food, even the odd book.

The bodies decreased in number. Geoffrey rounded a corner, and in triumph recognised the headteacher's door at the end of the corridor. The only thing which stood between him and it was a pair of boys marching shoulder to shoulder. The fact that they marched in step made them almost as menacing as the fact that they had made no concession to the school's uniform requirements. They were dressed in khaki trousers and green shirts, belted and booted like miniature infantrymen. For a moment Geoffrey wondered if the school had an army cadet corps. But Mr Springer was, he had been told, a pacifist. The pair came on without breaking step. He noticed that they carried between them a bulky black nylon bag. For a moment he thought they were going to barge him, but at the last moment they parted with military precision, the boy on the left taking the bag neatly from his companion. Without further incident Geoffrey reached his destination.

The room occupied by Mr L. Springer, B. Ed., was large

by the standards of the school, carpeted in durable squares
of man-made fibre in mud colour. Some of the squares had
worn a bit. A huge desk, a wall full of filing cabinets and
a table of computers filled the rest of the space. On the
wall was a blown-up aerial view of the school in black and
white. A single small shelf of paperbacks behind the desk
was the only concession to the academic life.

Amongst the fashionable litter, it was, at first, hard to
pick out the small figure of the head. He was sitting on the
front of the desk, his back to Geoffrey, his feet on his chair,
his ear clamped to a telephone.

'As far as I'm concerned that's a complete no-no.' He
paused without listening and went on. 'OK. OK, I hear
you. Look, I'm going to have to get back to you on this
one. I'm up to my eyes right now.'

He swung round to face Geoffrey, cradling the phone in
his lap. He reminded Geoffrey less of a teacher than of
some sort of guerrilla leader, fresh from jungle warfare
and only recently precipitated into civilian life. Springer
would have been happy to accept the description. He'd
worked hard at the image. Clothes, language, demeanour
– which he called 'body language'; nothing was accidental.
He'd started his professional life fifteen years earlier in
flannels and tweed jacket. Now his grey polo, black denims
and white trainers equipped him for the corridors of his
sort of power.

Or so he had thought. Recently, however, Springer had
begun to wonder if he had got it right. He had been trained
in education at a time when old goals were being deserted
and new, equally rigid ones put in place. When he had
entered the profession, academic ends for schools were
being abandoned and social work and interpersonal skills
were in. A basic diet of elementary sociology and

integrated sciences delivered cross-curricularly had been the fashion, and Springer was ever in touch with fashion; he had indeed, no other criterion for his selection of values. He had no vision of education as familiarity with the best in human achievement, only of socialisation, an ability to fit into a prevailing culture. But over the last couple of years his political masters had ceased to allow fashion, or indeed teachers, to continue down that route. The changes had hit the inner London area later than the rest of the country. Now they were here, however, Springer, for the first time in his career, was uncertain where the bandwagon lay.

He was, therefore, less at ease with Geoffrey than he would have liked. He couldn't quite make up his mind whether the Church might be useful to him or whether it was a hopeless back number ('a complete no-no'), association with which might mark him out for failure.

Ten years ago he'd thought he'd got the Church taped. It was useless to him. The odd West Indian baptist, a demure Chinese or two and a courteous Hindu he could cope with. Even the Turkish and Greek Cypriots had caused no problem. Then the Sikhs had come in force. The Muslims had followed. Suddenly he'd been less sure of his line.

Always alert to social change, never less than professional in his responses, he'd gone on a course and emerged an expert. He'd learnt the jargon and told his secretary to rename the ethnic minorities files 'multi-cultural'. By the time they'd been ready to computerise the records, the roll was thirty per cent multi-cultural. At times Springer felt all this was a bit unfair. He'd been trained to attend to all types of deprivation: cultural, linguistic, economic, emotional. But the multi-cultural communities didn't seem quite to fit into his categories of deprivation. They had a dignity, a culture, a set of skills which at times seemed almost threatening. Still, he was young yet. If the name of the game was making changes in the menus of school dinners, he was up to that.

But he'd been shaken, he had to admit, by a pretty terrible session with an ancient and very strong-looking Sikh who, through his grandson as interpreter – a bright lad in the ninth year who'd clearly enjoyed his role – had intimated he was not happy about assemblies. Springer thought he'd placated him by pointing out that there weren't that many held. This apparently was what the grandfather was unhappy about. He wanted for his grandson – here he'd laid a hand on the lad's head in a gesture which Springer had only seen in the cinema – a place where God was honoured. Springer was genuinely shocked. Not long after that had come the 1988 Education Act with its quaint requirement about mainly Christian assemblies. It was all so unfair, Springer felt. In fact, he was still worried about the religion bit.

'Geoff, I reckon I need your help. I'm worried about the religion bit.'

Geoffrey raised an eyebrow. 'How can I help?'

'What we absolutely must do, top priority, is stop talking, stop thinking negatively, and start talking, start thinking positively.'

The heads' course had left its trace.

'Indeed.'

'What I'm really saying is, what we have here aren't problems.' Springer's voice dropped a tone and he sought steady eye contact. 'They're not even challenges.' He paused, 'They're *opportunities*. Do you hear me?' Geoffrey thought this was really rather an uncouth thing to ask until he realised that perhaps what Springer meant was, 'Do you take my deeper meaning?' though Geoffrey did not think that there was any very deep meaning in this prattle. Springer was simply manifesting anxiety symptoms, and Geoffrey was an expert in fielding and coping with those. His pity and sympathy were perfectly genuine.

'What have you in mind?'

Springer ceased to swing his legs from the desk on which he was sitting and dropped athletically fully six inches to the floor. Then he squatted down opposite Geoffrey's low chair, exactly on a level with him, swinging his arms inside his legs, reminding Geoffrey of a monkey.

'What we need is to positively affirm the identities of all our pupils, whatever their faith community.' He rattled this off – slogan rather than reflection.

Geoffrey had no trouble concurring with this, but Springer's tone was very serious, almost threatening, as though Geoffrey had dissented instead of agreeing with him.

'I'm in favour of religion,' said Geoffrey gently. And it was true. There were few religions with which Geoffrey did not feel in sympathy, detect the good in and welcome as the most curious, most valuable expressions of the human soul.

'I think my contacts with the Sikh and Muslim communities are strong enough to get in people to help with assemblies, if that's what you had in mind.'

'That's absolutely marvellous, Geoff,' Springer exclaimed with too much enthusiasm. 'But,' his tone dropped to a minatory note as though Geoffrey had made a serious but forgivable mistake, 'I have to remind you –' here he pointed a finger like General Haig in the recruiting poster – 'the new Education Act requires us to deliver assemblies which are "for the most part Christian".'

Geoffrey had had enough of this. 'I dare say I might manage that too, if you want.'

The head's relief was, for him, palpable. 'Great. Just great. I leave it with you then, Geoff,' he said, rapidly rising to his feet and reaching for his telephone again. 'Get Cherry to give you some dates and keep me in the picture.'

He seemed to see from Geoffrey's surprised expression that he was being peremptory.

'I'm up to my eyes just now. I keep telling these publisher boys I'm the one who makes the deadlines.' He gestured to the set of proofs spread out on his table. 'But they reckon they can't wait. See you. *Ciao.*'

Outside the cutting sleet was slanting evilly across the car park, attacking Geoffrey as though it would like to kill him. He'd nearly reached his bike, when Cherry caught up with him. She seized him by the arm in her agitation.

'Reverend Brighouse, can you come back? Please. There's been . . . There's a boy dead.'

CHAPTER THREE

Innocent Subjects

The hush which hung over St Veep's at two o'clock on Monday afternoon was as thick and heavy as the soup served at luncheon. In the distance a piano could be heard tinkling out some utterly appropriate afternoon music. Scarlatti, would it be, or Couperin? Theodora worked away methodically at the bibliography for her Oxbridge candidates in the corner of the staff common room. The late afternoon sun illuminated the polished mahogany of the working tables and caught the grey and pink rugs on the waxed floor. The view from the window at her back gave out on to a surprisingly large garden. Two well-grown blue cedars and a fringe of copper beeches enclosed a large lawn which, even at this time of the year, looked green and manicured. The two gravel paths which ran from the house to the shrubbery two hundred yards away were neatly raked, the basin in the middle glittered with khaki-coloured water.

Theodora fleetingly recalled the garden of the south London vicarage at which she was presently lodged. There the rough, tussocky grass contained many a hidden hazard: rotting wheelbarrows, abandoned bicycle parts and an ossuary of ancient grey dog bones with frayed ends. The feeling was of a municipal adventure playground recently abandoned. And indeed the last curate's youth club had had a vigorous hand in its air of devastation.

Theodora basked in the healing silence. She contemplated her lot: Dame Alicia had suggested six hours a week for two terms cramming a couple of sixth-formers who had conceived the curious wish to try for theology at Oxbridge, and two fifth-year classes. It would bring her into school two mornings and one afternoon a week. It would make it economically possible for her to continue her curacy at St Sylvester's Betterhouse without bankrupting the parish's finances. Geoffrey, embattled between the demands of his too-numerous parish and his too-porous church roof, had scarcely paused before giving his consent. 'Gift of God, dear,' he'd said briefly, as she'd caught him, just, in the vicarage hallway, to put the school's proposition to him.

'Shouldn't be surprised,' he said over his shoulder, 'if some of your youngsters didn't speak in complete sentences.'

His own group once a week at SWL comprehensive didn't do that on the whole. Not that he didn't love them, he'd told Theodora, but he noticed it had rendered his own teaching vocabulary narrower, more monosyllabic.

'Yes,' Theodora had replied to his retreating back as he took the stairs two at a time.

At five to four there was a light tap at the common-room door, then the rattle of crockery and the sound of wheels squeaking on the parquet and a maid in a black dress had backed into the room drawing a tea-trolley behind her. The cups were china. A couple of plates of fresh-looking scones invited on the lower tray. Theodora relished this spectacle. The maid smiled kindly. 'Shall I serve you, miss, or would you like to wait for the rest.'

'I'll wait,' murmured Theodora.

At four precisely, the discrete gong boomed in the hall. There was a moment's pause and then a subdued noise as of a dozen hives opened. Classes had ended. The staff returned.

Oenone Troutbeck, whose sense of drawing-room etiquette was second only to Miss Aldriche's of team management, converged on Theodora at the same moment. Oenone gracefully allowed her senior to bat first.

'How very nice to have you with us. It's good of you to help us out at this time in the term and at such short notice. We're awfully grateful to Barbara for finding you for us. Are you finding your way around?'

Miss Aldriche's manner was exactly right. She had been running things all her life. As the eldest child of a country doctor widowed early, she had run, first, her father and brother and sister. Later, as head girl, she had, naturally, run her school, and likewise, in due course, her college junior common room. Finally, as second mistress, it was averred by those in the know that, whatever the hierarchical niceties, it was she who ran the best girls' school in the country.

She had entered teaching because, at that time, it had offered power, scope for female talent and opportunities for scholarship. If she had been born a little later she would have run the country. Her expectations were that women would lead. She had no use for modern interpretations of feminism, finding their analyses of fundamental concepts insufficiently rigorous and at times too coloured by emotion. She herself never needed to insist. It was apparent that she was rational, intelligent, immensely competent and altruistic. She had, moreover, one extremely useful skill. As a modern historian with an interest in genealogy she had at least a scholarly acquaintance with most of the important families in England. She ranged widely; the more modern *noblesse* from journalism, politics and the media were as well known to her as the scions of nineteenth-century academic dynasties. So when Barbara Brighouse had said to her in her downright way, 'Mere is wasting his pupils' time,' Miss Aldriche had put her administrative mind to work out the permutations. It was not desirable that there should be a row with the clerical governors. What was wanted was a solid woman, academically competent, who could replace the Reverend Robert little by little almost before he himself had noticed it.

A little inquiry, the odd phone call to old college acquaintances, indeed a courteous sounding out of the episcopal governor, and finally Barbara Brighouse's acquaintance with her brother's curate, had discovered Theodora Braithwaite, granddaughter of an old girl whose portrait hung in the library, of impeccable clerical ancestry, possessing a respectable degree in Lit. Hum., just waiting to be scooped up.

So it was with genuine pleasure that she approached Theodora to welcome her into their midst. She had no misgivings.

'Thank you,' Theodora replied. 'Yes, people have been most kind.'

'Is this all very strange to you?' Oenone glided into the conversation, 'or are you – ' Theodora thought she was going to say 'one of us', but she ended – 'an old hand?'

Theodora took in Miss Troutbeck's appearance; much thought had been given in order to achieve great simplicity which had nothing of the peasant in it. There appeared to be a great deal of cashmere and Thai silk. 'I have taught a little but not quite at this level,' Theodora replied.

'Where would that have been?'

'Africa, Nairobi.'

'Really,' Oenone hadn't quite got enough to go on so she pressed on. 'Nairobi. Did you by any chance know the McDermotts there?'

'Yes. They were members of St Augustine's congregation.'

'Ah yes, of course. Were you there long?'

'I had three happy years.'

'You may have met my uncle, Henry.'

Theodora reviewed her acquaintance with the white community and recalled a rather jolly drunken retired diplomat who had diplomatically and drunkenly settled for the new regime. She nodded. 'Sir Henry was much about.'

Oenone appeared more or less satisfied. She became more expansive. 'What did you do out there?'

'I served my first curacy.'

Oenone was too well-bred to evince surprise. 'Really? You're in orders?'

'Deacons'. Yes.'

'Anglican?'

Theodora grinned. 'Is there anything else?'

Oenone now had to start all over again. 'And what are you doing at present?'

'Serving my second curacy at St Sylvester's Betterhouse.'

'So you'll be a priest in due course?'

'No, I think not.'

'Isn't it rather a cul-de-sac then, being a perpetual curate?'

Theodora forbore to speak of vocation. Instead she said

mildly, 'It has its rewards. Such as a part-time teaching post here.'

Barbara Brighouse, who had seized and downed her first cup of tea and got to her second scone, strode up, with Miss King at her heels. A red setter and a Jack Russell, Theodora thought.

'Theo, my dear, it is good to see you. I'm so glad Geoffrey felt he could spare you from that dreadful parish of his.' Her manner clearly indicated a previous acquaintance.

Theodora felt both loyalty and love for St Sylvester's, but before she could respond to Miss Brighouse, Miss King broke in. 'I expect you'll want to meet our chaplain. Only he doesn't seem to be around at the moment. I almost feel at times he avoids the common room.' Miss King's malicious little grey eyes in her little round face went with a low, melodious voice, rather more powerful than might be expected from her small frame.

Theodora hadn't realised that the school had a chaplain. Barbara, briefly visiting her priestly brother to look over Theodora, had made no allusion to one. He had not been mentioned by Dame Alicia at their brief interview either. She knew instantly that she would threaten any chaplain. If he'd been any good she would not have been appointed.

Barbara bounded into the breach. 'You really ought to see your grandmother's stuff, I believe you said you hadn't seen the portrait of her as a young woman.'

Theodora was quite ready to let people off hooks. 'No, I haven't seen it. My Uncle Hugh mentioned it. What's it like?'

'Chocolate box,' said Miss King, baulked of her prey and therefore angry. 'But there are bits of classical stuff which she got on her travels in the Near East between the wars.

There's the Nike at the top of the stairs, and a relief of a male standing figure clasping a spear which derives, I do not know at what distance, from a second-century temple relief in Sicily.' Miss King was classically exact. 'Also one or two bits of the male physique in the studio, under lock and key.'

'Why lock and key?' Theodora inquired, startled.

'Drawing from the living male nude is not yet quite acceptable here, but Cromwell likes his examination candidates to have some chance to draw the male figure, so the Braithwaite Bequest's antique plastercast is regarded as a reasonable compromise.' Miss Brighouse was dry. 'Personally I can't see why they don't take them down to the Slade and let them do it properly.'

'Perhaps that would be a little daring,' said Mrs Gulland, who had come up to join the group.

Oenone was busily adding up the score 'You're Lady Helena Braithwaite's granddaughter then?' Her relief was palpable. One of us.

Theodora nodded. 'My paternal grandmother was a pupil here, yes.'

It looked as though Oenone's interrogation might start all over again, but Barbara Brighouse had had enough. 'I think this might be quite a good moment for me to show you round. There's that portrait of your grandmother by Laslo, and a good collection of books and manuscripts, including her diary of her travels in Greece and Turkey,' she said, rapidly propelling Theodora before her.

They had not quite reached the common-room door when it opened and one of the three indistinguishable mathematicians flung it open wide and, briefcase in one hand, gloves in the other, said in a voice which had been useful to her as a house captain at Roedean, 'Dame Alicia would like you all to remain here. One of our pupils has been kidnapped and the police will need to see everyone.'

Even so, Theodora got back to St Sylvester's before Geoffrey. She let herself into the dark hall of the immense Victorian vicarage just before eight o'clock. The tessellated floor echoed to footsteps as she shook out her raincoat and hung it on the stand. There was evidence of other occupants in a dozen damp coats which the stand accommodated easily. A murmur of voices from the large door on the right indicated that the evening's religious business was in hand. Theodora, who knew better than to use the light switch, made her way unerringly down the bare basement steps to her own flat.

She had inherited the flat from the previous curate whose tastes had run to the mechanical and she was still discovering tools the names of which she did not know at the back of the ample cupboards. The flat had its own entrance directly on to the street, but Geoffrey seemed not to mind her using the vicarage front door and, since this was more convenient, that was what she did.

Ten minutes later, Theodora heard Geoffrey's feet scraping on the front door boot-scraper. She heard him hesitate and then walk across the hall. A moment later she opened her door to his characteristic tap. Theodora produced excellent bacon sandwiches, pushed the mustard in Geoffrey's direction, and poured thick sweet Indian tea into two mugs, on the side of which was emblazoned, 'St Sylvester's Centenary Appeal 1877–1977.'

'What's up?' Theodora inquired.

Geoffrey told her.

'So it was an accident?'

'Well, there'll have to be an inquest but the place is

being rewired. It looks as though the workmen left the electricity switched on. The boy shouldn't have been in the room and of course the workmen are swearing they secured the door. But . . .'

'Are you seeing the parents, or would you like me to?'

'Thanks. I've seen everyone, I think. Mother, though not father, police, staff, head, LEA officer, very worried.'

'About insurance', Theodora surmised.

Geoffrey smiled wanly. 'What else?'

'Who was the boy? Anyone you know?'

'Yes, Paul Kostas.'

Theodora raised an eyebrow. 'Oh dear. How about Kostas's father?' Theodora knew the family only by repute. Geoffrey had spoken of the boys, other parishioners knew some of the adults in that tough family. They were a large clan of Greeks whose place in local respect was assured partly by their resources (most of the men drove Mercedes) and partly by their aggression. There had been a recent court case, she seemed to remember; something to do with GBH against a neighbour. One of the Kostases had done six months in consequence, apparently.

'Mother was evasive,' said Geoffrey. 'I think she doesn't know where he is.'

'Still inside?'

'No. The efficient headmaster knew he'd been out three weeks.'

'What about the twin?'

'He's silent. In a family of two sisters, a mother, a grandmother and some sort of aunt or cousin, all giving tongue to grief, he's silent. As a family, of course, they're close, and that will help; but on the other hand they'd like to make someone a scapegoat. I fear it may be the headmaster or perhaps the chap in charge of the group at the time.'

'Who was?'

'A fellow called Ralph Troutbeck. English and drama specialist. He doesn't seem to have all that much control over the group. They appear to have been wandering around a bit.'

'Troutbeck. An unusual name. There's a Troutbeck at St Veep's. Rather insistently well bred. Quizzing newcomers like me.' She paused. 'And we too have not been without incident at the establishment across the water.' Theodora recapitulated on the happenings.

'Do they know why the child was kidnapped?'

'She's the daughter of a Greek diplomat. Mother's English. The chauffeur drives her in daily in a bullet-proof Mercedes. It was assumed that Mercs at the Greek embassy are all bullet-proofed, but of course now they're wondering if there was a reason.'

'I suppose the place is crawling with police?'

Theodora nodded. 'Rather more than turned out for your sad little affair.'

Geoffrey had mentioned the squad car of a sergeant and a constable followed by a police ambulance. St Veep's had had four plainclothes men, two dark, mustachioed security men with strong accents and an inspector.

He glanced curiously at Theodora. 'And how is my sister coping?'

'Need you ask? Splendidly. Barbara's enjoying it rather. You are an admirable family, Geoffrey.'

Geoffrey smiled his delighted smile. It cleared his face from ear to ear.

'Aren't we?'

'It's terrible for the family though, and one hates to think of the girl. They're trying to keep it out of the papers in case of a ransom demand, a request with which Dame

38

Alicia's only too happy to concur. I gather she's rather thrown by something as eminently newsworthy as a kidnapping. She's been used to getting prime-time publicity for St Veep's at any price. Now that she could have it for free, pressed down and running over, she doesn't want it. I think the notion of bad publicity for St Veep's up to now has been oxymoronic. It'll be interesting to see how she copes. Did you know, by the way, my Uncle Hugh married Dame Alicia?'

'Surely not?'

'It was long before she was known, of course. Hugh had a parish in Portsmouth at the time. Pound was something young and glamorous in the Navy – naval attaché? Something of the sort. Perhaps you knew of them?'

Theodora always gave full weight to Geoffrey's naval network.

Geoffrey shook his head. 'Is he still about?'

'Killed in an air crash in Africa about ten years ago. I rather think he and Dame Alicia'd followed their own paths for some time before it happened.'

'What a lot you know.'

Theodora sat up full in her chair. 'I think it counts as pastoral skill.'

'You could put it like that. Do you keep a card index?'

Theodora was genuinely hurt. 'You don't seem to realise what's involved in the clerical web,' she said earnestly, taking a determined bite of the last bacon sandwich. 'Of course, both you and I have family, school and university networks, but you must remember my lot have been clerical now for eight generations. You're the first of your family in the priesthood. It mounts up, you know, more than masonic. There can't be many parts of England Braithwaites haven't at some time served in. What I lack, and rather envy you, is the services connection. That would help.'

'No chaplains?'

'To tell you the truth', Theodora said apologetically, 'we rather looked down on them as a breed. Like temporary gentlemen in the First World War.'

'I'm sorry,' Geoffrey conceded. 'I've had too much contact with the caring professions today. They all work off card indexes. Or, in the case of Lance Springer, computer records. I don't know why I feel it's more humane to trust to memory.' He shrugged. 'After all, one can widen one's scope and be more accurate with a database.'

Theodora shook her head. 'Numbers are not important and we, by which I mean the Church should aim at quality not quantity. After all, we're not aiming to offer quite the same sorts of thing as the social services. As for accuracy, no computer I've yet dealt with matches my Uncle Hugh.'

The sound of voices and the clatter of feet on the hall floor above them announced the break-up of the parish meeting. Geoffrey lurched to his feet. 'I must go and say a kind word to encourage Henry before he goes.'

He hurled the remains of his mug of tea down his throat as though it were vodka, and shot up the short flight of shallow steps to the ground floor. The most contained, the most modest of priests, his only excess was a certain histrionicism in his bodily movements. It was as though the fact that he was tall and red-haired evoked excessive expectations in people which his generosity did not like to disappoint but which his own balanced nature deprecated. The drama of gesture and posture, Theodora reflected, was his way of satisfying people whilst protecting his inner reserve. She watched the hot water splash over the plates. She'd been right to take the curacy. She was at ease with Geoffrey and he, she felt, with her. He cared about people in the right way, respecting them, leaving them space to choose. She could learn from him. Might he have anything to learn from her?

The telephone shrilled in the basement an hour later. Theodora pushed aside Mowinkel on the Psalms and reached for the instrument. Geoffrey, she knew from the sounds of doors closing and murmured voices, was engaged in the study.

'Miss Braithwaite . . . Theodora, if I may. I am so very sorry to intrude at this rather late hour, but I really need to have a word. Barbara seemed to think that you keep late hours in your parish.'

Miss Aldriche's pleasant low voice with its admirable enunciation of the language came clearly into the basement flat.

'How can I help?' Theodora was sleepy but willing.

'It's the Stephanopoulos girl of course. The one who was kidnapped.'

'Yes?'

'I naturally had a word with her mama, after the police had finished.'

'Yes.'

'I'm really rather worried about her. I wondered . . .?'

'Of course I'll go and see her.' Theodora's pastoral instinct never failed.

'Oh, if you could. We would be so very grateful. I rather paved the way for you. Family connection and so on.'

Theodora was nonplussed. 'What?'

'Well, your grandmother and Stella Stephanopoulos's mother were both old girls.' Miss Aldriche was triumphant. 'So of course the history of the foundation as well as its present reputation is dear to her and to you too, I imagine.'

'Naturally'. Theodora was guarded.

There was a pause. 'What I mean is, Dame Alicia is anxious—'

'I can well understand it.'

'—that there shouldn't be any . . .'

She now knew exactly to what Miss Aldriche was referring. 'Mrs Stephanopoulos might break it to the press, blame the school? Something of that sort?'

'She's naturally distraught.'

'When would you advise I call?'

'I ventured to suggest tomorrow morning.'

Theodora couldn't help but admire the lack of grass growing beneath the senior ladies' feet.

'They have an embassy flat in Church Row, Hampstead. I said about ten-thirty?

Geoffrey never, after all, reached the deserving Henry. The doorbell rang as he gained the hall. Swerving in his course, Geoffrey beheld in the porch the tiny, black-clad figure of Mrs Kostas. He drew her gently inside.

'Father, my husband,' she began, 'I cannot find him. He is . . .'

'Come into the study, Mrs Kostas.' Geoffrey's manner effortlessly conveyed warmth and formal courtesy and the woman, who had clearly been weeping, repossessed herself.

CHAPTER FOUR

Innocent Objects

On Tuesday morning Stella Stephanopoulos heard the bell almost before it rang. She was standing in front of her bedroom mirror and, with a gesture which looked studied but was in fact, after years of indulgence, quite automatic, she smoothed her auburn hair back from her broad brow. The bedroom, its pieces de résistance a turquoise padded bedhead, and one complete wall faced with pink mirror-glass, faced south and caught the morning sun. The room had an air of a child playing at Hollywood.

Stella had missed the thirties but they had been her mother's time. There were photographs on glass-topped tables and in morocco-covered albums. A great deal of furniture was in glass and chrome. Shagreen cases, the remnants of make-up in old crocodile handbags, even clothes in fabrics no longer known – tussore, gros grain – all these she had inherited from her mother. She had recognised her spiritual medium, seized it and enhanced it. Fox furs, silver and red, gleamed with artificial eyes out of the top of her wardrobe. The accoutrements from a past and, therefore, safer age, gave Stella the courage to inhabit her own period.

The last of a large family born to old parents, she had herself married late and, as it were, kept up the tradition. She had been an old-fashioned girl, but racy, fast driving as the thirties had allowed women to be. She was a minia-ture, pretty beyond words; not handsome, but every last bit of her made the best of. In her person, as in her drawing room, wherever the eye went, it was delighted and sur-prised. Bijou was a word that was heard of her, while her setting was decorated, illustrated almost, with plants, pictures, hangings. Her daughter, her only child – where was she now? – was destined, she hoped, to inherit it all.

Now the bell pealed in the Georgian cottage. The house did not really suit her adopted style. There was a tension she recognised but made no attempt to solve. It was a problem, she understood, for her audience, not for the actress herself. She descended the two floors, her tiny feet tapping and navigating the narrow staircase, its rickety turns testing her high-heeled balance, which did not fail her. The maid reached the door before her but the security man anticipated them both. His massive back and thick, sleeked-back hair made a formidable outline as he stood framed in the cottage door and looked up into Theodora's level and courteous gaze.

'*Ti*?' he inquired.

'Theodora Braithwaite. I have an appointment with Mrs Stephanopoulos.'

'Do come in.' Characters in novels cry. Rarely so in real life. Stella Stephanopoulos, Theodora noted, cried. Her deep thrilling voice with its clipped thirties vowels cried. The security man, however, failed to give way. His squat, solid form remained in place.

'*Oriste?*'

Mrs Stephanopoulos resorted to syntactically perfect but English-accented Greek, and he stepped nimbly aside and came to attention. Theodora smiled at him and remarked his elegant moustaches. The dog, a Staffordshire bull terrier, brindle and white, stood dead centre in the middle of the hall like a sailor on a swaying deck, his feet placed wide apart and braced, his tail straight out behind him, a shark-like smile slashed across his face. Theodora nodded to him in a comradely fashion. He thumped his tail but, like the man, did not budge. This time Mrs Stephanopoulos resorted to peremptory English and he swung sideways to allow the two women to shake hands.

'Miss Braithwaite, I am so enormously pleased to see you.'

Theodora stooped her head to enter the small front door and emerged into the white-painted, panelled hall. Her eye took in a niche with a wooden madonna, her beechwood robes fluttering, her honest peasant face smiling in delight as she displayed in the crook of her arm the infant Christ to a world which, she was confident, would want to admire him. At the feet of the statue stood a small table with a silver salver and its litter of cards, invitations, advertisements, like votive offerings. For a moment Theodora's eye rested on a familiar-looking card. Then she followed her hostess upstairs. In the drawing room on the first floor, a toy fire glowed in the minuscule iron grate. The room ran from the front of the house to the back, with something of a curve round the chimney breast in the centre. Seventeenth-century walnut glowed, eighteenth-century silver glittered. Stella Stephanopoulos graced the room. There might well be resources for a ransom here, Theodora reflected.

'It is good of you to come. I, George, and I are . . .' She

stopped. Suddenly the actress failed.

'Have you had any news?' Theodora asked gently.

'Nothing. The police tell us nothing.' She searched around for comfort, 'Konstantin, the ambassador, has been so kind to George, to both of us. He phoned yesterday twice. The second time in person. He said we could call on any of the embassy's resources. The security men and so on. But it's all a bit late.' Theodora glanced over Stella's head. Above the fireplace hung a three-quarter portrait of a man in army uniform. He was fresh-complexioned with sleek fair hair brushed back from a high forehead. The face was large, and square, the grey eyes which met the spectator's were cold and level. Major George Stephanopoulos, was inscribed in black letters on the small gilt plaque at the bottom of the frame. He looked less Greek than German, Theodora thought and not so much competent as ruthless. She turned her attention back to her hostess.

'Do you know how it actually happened?'

'Michel, our driver, takes her to St Veep's from here about the same time every day and picks her up after school.'

'Michel is . . .?'

'He opened the door to you. He's on the permanent staff in this country. He has British nationality. Before he picks her up she's supposed to wait inside the school in the entrance hall – on the marble, as they call it – until he rings. You know St Veep's of course?'

'I know its reputation, of course. But in fact I only started teaching there yesterday. I'm learning.'

'Of course, I was there myself.' Stella smiled wanly. 'It hasn't changed. Physically, I mean, or in ethos. I think they've sharpened it up academically. There's a porter, in fact the same man who was there in my day. Root, I think he's called. He's always in the entrance hall, so there shouldn't be any gap when she's alone. But on this occasion she was late for some reason, and she came out of the side entrance. The kidnap car was parked somewhere near Michel's and she reached it first. Apparently it was rather like ours. A black Mercedes. Just one man inside. There was no struggle. She didn't scream or anything. Perhaps she was too surprised.'

'How do you know all this?'

'A Veepian, a sixth-former, Clarissa Bennet I think she was called; she came out just after Jessica and saw it all. She wasn't sure what was happening. Then she saw Michel, put two and two together and raised the alarm. There was no violence. Not even a kerfuffle. I gather it was about ten minutes before everyone realised what had happened and another ten before the police arrived.

'Twenty minutes for them to be gone in.'

Stella's tears, which had been kept at bay by her concentration on the facts she was reciting, now coursed down her face.

'Do you know, can you guess who or why?'

Finally Stella said, 'There's nothing. We have – ' she glanced round – 'nothing.'

Theodora followed her glance with raised eyebrow. Stella smiled a forgiving moue of a smile. 'I mean, comparatively. George isn't a ship-owner. He's a soldier. The house is mostly embassy issue. One or two things of my family's. But as a ransom, surely not worth while.'

'The Greek government?'

'Are hardly going to shell out for the daughter of a military attaché.'

'Are you certain it was a political kidnapping?'

47

Stella shrugged pathetically. 'What else could it be? The car. The planning. The timing. It wasn't casual.'

'Hence your Mercedes with toughened glass?'

'It's partly prestige. Anyone at the level of attaché tends to get toughened glass. Many military don't feel safe outside armoured cars, anyway. Not that George is like that at all. He's brave as a lion but, yes, he's done his bit, of course, and has his enemies like others in the Greek army officer class.'

'So revenge is a possibility, you would guess?'

'It's what I – we – fear most.'

'Can you pin down the revenge motive, I mean, to particular episodes?' Theodora could hardly ask what horrors George had perpetrated in his time and to whom.

Mrs Stephanopoulos turned in her tiny armchair so that she was facing Theodora. There was a momentary pause and Theodora's refined pastoral sense detected a change of emotional tone. Whether it was going to lead to greater honesty or merely another change of scene, time would tell.

Eventually the longing to unburden herself to a safe source won. The solidity, the sheer goodness of generations of competent Anglican clerics drew Stella Stephanopoulos. 'You must understand that Greek politics and, indeed, Greek society is not at all like English,' she began. 'Did you read classics by any chance?'

Theodora nodded.

'Of course. Well, it's all much more like Homer with the nastier bits of Thucydides thrown in.'

'Power and honour the main motives?'

'Which, when they're actually experienced at close quarters, look, feel much more like brutality and arrogance. Not that George is brutal, but his family has been reasonably successful. They come from the north, Macedonia. They were prominent in the 1840s, repelling the Turks in the war of independence. Later they did quite well under the monarchy. The family was pretty comfortable. George's father, Andreas, could afford to live off inherited income. He collected, mostly Byzantine stuff, dealt a little, was something of a scholar. When the Nazis walked in in May 1941, they were all massively unprepared. Andreas's mother, George's grandmother, had been German originally, something to do with the court-in-waiting, something like that. I think he thought it might be all right. He . . .' Stella hesitated. 'Andreas didn't quite fight the Germans. He tried to get the family out of the country and didn't manage it. George was born in 1938, so he says he hardly remembers the war, but it was undoubtedly tough. The Nazis arrested Andreas in '41 and George didn't see his father for two years. While he was away, George's mother died of septacaemia. There were simply no medicines, you see.'

Theodora reviewed the bits of this tale which had been left unsaid: a German grandmother; a difficult time; a father who didn't quite fight but then ended in a German prison camp; a needy, motherless family used to riches and not quite having them. Were there tensions there which, a generation later, could lead to kidnapping?

'George's father, Jessica's grandfather, is he still alive?' Theodora asked.

'Andreas died in '84. Heart attack.'

'Then why should anyone want to take revenge on his granddaughter?'

'There was too much money,' Stella said with a rush, 'and he got out too early.'

Theodora was puzzled. 'You mean?'

'The Germans let grandfather out of prison in '43. Too

49

early. And after the war he had enough money to go into politics. Not a cheap matter in Greece anyway, if you weren't of the left, which of course, Andreas wasn't.'

'You mean he might have dealt with the Nazis in some way?'

Stella shrugged her tiny shrug. 'We've never discussed it. It would be very painful to someone of George's temperament. He is the soul of honour, you understand . . . Any stain of that kind would be unendurable for him.'

Faced with such a cul-de-sac. Theodora could only try again. 'Is there anything which your husband is aware of which could lead to the abduction of his daughter? I mean, whatever her family have or have not done, surely hurting the child is barbaric.'

'Oh my dear,' Stella's fine brown eyes turned to Theodora. 'I'm sure you are classicist enough to know it's practically a tradition in Greece.'

'Had she,' Theodora explored fresh ground, 'any intimation, do you think, that she was in danger?'

'I don't know how much children of that age pick up about their position in life. She's been brought up internationally. She was born in Athens, and we were in Cyprus when the Turkish thing blew up; we all left rather quickly. After that we did a spell in the States. It was supposed to be full of crime, but in fact I found it rather restful after the Near East. Living here, of course – ' Mrs Stephanopoulos spread her hands to indicate the security of London – 'we tend to suppose we're safe.'

'What sort of a girl is Jessica?' Theodora stopped herself saying 'was' in time.

Stella's voice broke and Theodora, previously alienated by the theatre and the props, melted in pity for the woman. 'She was terribly ordinary. Much more English than Greek.

Of course we've always had English, or anyway, Scottish nannies, and she really isn't outstanding in any way.'

Mrs Stephanopoulos made ordinariness sound like a virtue which, Theodora thought, given her husband's rackety family, she was justified in doing. She turned to the table behind her. On it was a silver-framed black and white photograph of the head and shoulders of a girl. It was so small that Theodora had missed it. She had the feeling it did not usually stand in that place. It was too small and too intimate. She looked into the face of a girl of about fourteen, fair straight hair scraped severely back from a broad brow, a thin face, deep-set eyes which considered the observer, returned their gaze and gave nothing away. An ordinary face, as her mother had said, but perhaps distinguished by a hint of strength, Theodora thought. Round Jessica's neck she could see a small Greek cross.

'She was going through a religious phase just now,' Mrs Stephanopoulos said. 'That's quite normal for fourteen-year-olds, isn't it?' Stella sought Theodora's expert reassurance in such matters. 'It made her a little bit secretive. I think she felt that her father didn't approve. I suppose she was right in a way. George feels religion is part of the state apparatus, it keeps the peasants happy but it's not for the intelligent. He didn't like the idea of a devout daughter. Her grandfather, Andreas, wanted her to be Orthodox but I felt it would be safer to have her confirmed as an Anglican so she joined the class at St Veep's. She's to be done at Easter.'

Theodora felt she was getting nowhere. 'Could we see her room?' she asked on an impulse.

Theodora squeezed round the narrow staircase behind the slim form of Mrs Stephanopoulos to the third, the attic floor. The room was small and unexpectedly elegant for a girl of fourteen. There was a total absence of photographs of pop stars. Instead there were white walls, a grey carpet and pink curtains, a smell of pot-pourri and a glimpse of St Mary's Church Row from the single window. A solid mahogany bookshelf reached the ceiling on the wall opposite the window. On the other wall opposite the bed was a tallboy on which stood what Theodora recognised as an icon case in chased silver, its doors folded back. It was a picture of the Virgin and child. The calm, austere face of the Virgin was turned towards the front and her son raised his hand in blessing on her arm. The icon was flanked by two silver candles. Theodora noticed that the candles in the sticks were new but that both wicks were blackened.

'A beautiful thing,' Theodora murmured. She wondered what terrors Jessica had repelled by meditation on such an object.

'Her grandfather, Andreas, gave it to her before he died. It's not valuable but she seems very fond of it.'

It was the icon which stayed with Theodora as she drove home from the unsatisfactory visit. We're surrounded every day by artifacts which remind us of heaven, the kingdom of God, the other world, she reflected as she sped downhill from Hampstead to Betterhouse. Spires, crosses, statues, icons, architecture, language itself, our society is saturated with these angelic voices. Why do we not heed them?

CHAPTER FIVE

Parish Life

Geoffrey loped the hundred yards from the vicarage to the church. He'd seen members of his youth club vault the gravestones, and felt envy that a cassock prevented his following suit. He swerved round the south side of the building and kicked with minimum force the bottom of the wooden door. A smell of Rentokil mixed with old incense met him. In the nave a cement mixer turned like some musical instrument as its load thudded quietly from one side to the other. He'd grown fond of the cement mixer. On Sundays the builders put a tarpaulin over it, in case it should offend the congregation. In the choir there were scaffold poles and piles of sand. Mixing boards provided stepping stones from presbytery to pulpit. To get to the pulpit was a gymnastic feat which both Geoffrey and his congregation relished. On the first occasion, he had leaped the trestles, ducked under the polythene sheeting, and manhandled a cement bag. He'd been rewarded by a round of applause from those attending the family eucharist. Theodora had remarked afterwards that he must find his naval training a great resource.

It suited Geoffrey, he had to admit. He'd be sorry when everything was shipshape, the physical challenge receded, and he was left with a building fit only to be used for formal worship.

Geoffrey had a strong sense of place. He had chosen Betterhouse for his first living quite as much as Betterhouse's PCC and the Watermen's Company, who were its patrons, had chosen him. When he had completed his curacy and the time had come for him to seek his first living, he'd prayed, reflected, and then rung an old friend of his in the Automobile Association. They'd gone up in his helicopter and circled London. The helicopter was noisy: speech was impossible. As they reached Gravesend, Geoffrey had gestured towards the Thames and mouthed, 'Can we follow it?' Harry Gunn had nodded assent and they had followed the ever-narrowing silver and khaki strip in the late afternoon light of a fine July day.

Geoffrey had surveyed the river frontage from Tilbury to Barnes. What stood out was not the railways or the banks but the churches: Wren and Hawkesmore, Gibbes and Street, classical and gothic revival, pointed their sharp spires, their balanced and confident towers, upward to the heavens. Woolwich, the Dogs, Deptford, Limehouse, Wapping and Southwark, Geoffrey's gaze swept from north to south banks as they choppered on.

'I think,' he'd resolved, 'I'll have one of those.'

In the event it was St Sylvester's Betterhouse, a huge gothic revival church on the south bank, upstream from Lambeth, that had fallen vacant. The Watermen's Company were not averse to having an ex-naval man in charge.

Geoffrey's predecessor, Canon Langthorne, clerical grandson of the clerical builder of the original church in the 1870s, had had to spend the greater part of his increasingly frail energies striving to keep the roof watertight. The battle against the elements had been an unequal one. The roof had continued to leak and the congregation, unvisited, untaught, unsupported in the ordinary crises of life, faced only with demands for money which they did not have, had petered out, claimed by death or accidie.

Geoffrey knew that people, even religious people, need the concrete. Buildings and artefacts are necessary to nourish sanctity in the midst of the terrors of an unholy world: just as we can't keep upright as human beings without institutions, traditions, systems and networks, so we can't manage to progress in the spiritual life without holy places and holy things. Geoffrey's evangelical brother clergy who were wont to proclaim that people were more important than buildings, had underestimated the potency of place and time and overestimated the ability of sheep to sustain religious patterns of living without frequent reminders. To create, to maintain a Christian culture we need help, Geoffrey reflected, wheresoever we can get it.

The building of St Sylvester's Betterhouse had been designed explicitly to provide such help and such reminders. It stood on the edge of the parish, its spire visible still from every part of it. At its back, behind the vicarage, the Thames flowed. The church's architecture was extreme enough to merit mention in the guides on gothic revival. It had been designed by a rich priest for a poor area. He had spent his fortune on it and it had left him nobly and happily poor. He had taken his time and not been afraid to change his mind. A pupil of Street had entered into the spirit of the thing, and designed everything from steeple to door-hinges, to symbolise and remind the congregation of the great Christian truths. Every sort of material had been used to celebrate the diversity of creation: marble, brick, stone, encaustic tiles, tesseral and glass were meant to remake the medieval in patterns arranged to bring the worshipper to his knees. The effect was, as Canon Langthorne had wished, overwhelming. In the enormous nave saints leaned from their niches between the clerestory windows, urging upon the worshipper the message of the gospel.

Alas, as the century after the first foundation stones were laid wore on, those very features which had aimed to attract and uplift the ordinary people of Betterhouse began to mystify, frighten and repel them. Geoffrey was aware that few of his parishioners understood the building's symbolism, or its aids to safe living. He acknowledged he had much to do. He was determined that the pattern of his own ministry should be different from that of his predecessor. And he'd been fortunate. The bishop had retired, the Watermen had produced funds, his own energy had been matched by that of an archdeacon. The renewed building, its roof tight against the elements, had begun to emerge from its long slumber.

He gazed down the length of the enormous nave, built to seat five hundred at the height of the church-going 1870s, before the car had destroyed Sunday observance. Far away in front of him, five steps led up to the high altar, a stone table with a daunting gilt reredos at its back. 'Be ye high and lifted up', said the psalmist. Well, the altar on its sacred mountain always had that effect on Geoffrey. It achieved its purpose. It quelled, it dominated, it made one think of quite other things than everyday life. Places, Geoffrey knew, form and constrain conduct. He had served on large ships and small ones, helicopters so cramped you put your crew's eye out by too sudden a movement, and transports so large you could hold a dance in them. But of all his working environments, Geoffrey loved this one, his first church, the best.

'You will be coming for your prayers,' said a voice high up on his left.

Geoffrey caught sight of the beautifully turbaned and bearded head of the building foreman six foot up on the scaffolding between the organ pipes and the high altar.

'No, Mr Singh, I'm just going to sort the boot sale stuff in the vestry. I won't disturb you.'

'You never disturb us, Reverend Geoffrey,' Mr Singh replied tranquilly, and withdrew his face between the scaffold poles like a green man retiring into his foliage.

When the builders had first taken possession of the church the previous autumn, Geoffrey had talked about having to work round them. He's spoken in this way to Theodora, new to the parish but not to parish ways. But he'd been wrong. They'd taught him to work not round them but with them. They were a gang based on the family principle. Mr Singh had originally worked for an old local family, Makepeace Brothers, who'd reached bankruptcy in the 1980s. They had been saved by the immigrant influx of which Mr Singh and his family were examples. Mr Singh had started in a dignified way mixing cement by hand and patiently handing bricks to a young cockney. The cockney had broken his neck one rainy night when his motorcycle misjudged a bollard, and Mr Singh had taken his place. In time Mr Singh had introduced his cousin, an accountant, to the firm; his nephews, Mr Mahood and Mr Talwar, followed after a decent interval. They worked with a sort of rhythmic, dependable precision. In their private life they helped to found and supported the local gurdwara. They were sober, reliable and quick to learn. They bought out the last of the ailing Makepeace brothers. The firm prospered.

To Geoffrey they were a delight. When the archdeacon had told him that the faculty had been granted and the money found to repair and refurbish St Sylvester's, he'd been particularly eager that those responsible for the work should not be the usual building-site force, shouting their monotonous obscenities from one end of the church to the other, careless of atmosphere and artefacts. Makepeace and Singh had been just right. The courteous brown faces of the Singh cousinhood could be seen peering sympathetically through the foliage of scaffold planks and electric leads. If he came about lunch-time he could find them in the south aisle near the lady chapel, unobtrusively cooking on a neat iron brazier which seemed to fit naturally into the ecclesiastical setting.

'Please be seated, Reverend Geoffrey,' Mr Singh the eldest had said formally on the first occasion he had happened upon them, 'and do us the honour to eat with us.'

Geoffrey had been much moved, had shared a chapatti and a curried marrow with them, and felt the Anglican church well served by its workforce.

He was well served too, he reckoned, by his curate. When the archdeacon had indicated that the money might stretch to one, provided he shared with the Foundation of St Sylvester next door to the church, he'd been surprised and gratified to find that Theodora, the only applicant for the post, shared many of his own views.

'Why here?' he'd asked her.

Theodora, who thought that if you really had a vocation you should let Providence choose your future for you, had been tempted to answer, 'Why not here?' But she was honest: she had a reason; indeed two reasons. 'We lived not far from the source of the Thames when I was a child. It's interesting in later years to see what it becomes. Also, of course, there's the Foundation of St Sylvester.'

Geoffrey had thought he understood. The Foundation of St Sylvester was the result of the late-nineteenth-century's wish to establish Catholic parishes in the urban developments of England. Its originator, the Reverend Thomas Henry Newcome, had been a follower of the Tractarian movement when at Oxford. His private fortune had enabled him to found an order of priests dedicated to the extension of Catholic life and teaching within the Anglican Church. Their aim was not the sudden conversion of the missionary or the evangelist, but the creation of an environment in which people could grow gradually into the Christian life through the discipline of prayer and sacrament. Two houses had been established for training priests and the refreshment of like-minded laymen, in Yorkshire and London. Langthorne had been willing to have the London house next to his church, and so they stood today linked by an asphalt path and a line of chestnut trees.

The fortunes of the order had fluctuated as Catholic bishops alternated with evangelical ones. But in the eighties of our own century, there had been a resurgence of interest in the connection of physical to spiritual. Doctors and psychiatrists had been recruited into the order, and the network had produced work which was interesting at the level of research as well as innovative in pastoral and parochial ministry. The present warden of the London house was the Reverend Gilbert Racy, a doctor, a psychiatrist and deeply suspect to the more mundane of his south London brother clergy.

It might well be, Geoffrey surmised, that someone coming to the Anglican ministry *de novo*, like Theodora, would be attracted by working under the aegis of such a priest. In this, however, Geoffrey was mistaken. Theodora had known about parochial ministry at its very best from the days of her childhood. She had seen and, as she grew, wholeheartedly admired her late father's parish service. What attracted Theodora to the Foundation was simply that the London house of St Sylvester possessed the archive for the Society. Theodora, a budding church historian, felt there might be scope for her talent.

Geoffrey had wanted a curate to help him build up the parish, and the only way to do that was to visit. Theodora visited. From tower block to Victorian terrace she fought her way through dogs and children, becoming daily a familiar figure to the parish. He'd found her totally committed and surprisingly able to deal with a wide social variety. She had an unfussy competence which sprang, he supposed, from her clerical family. He suspected that she made lists and kept to them. She was prayerful and not apparently too worried about the question of women's priesting. He had the impression she felt it was a waste of energy, perhaps indeed a temptation, to dwell on that issue. He had no objection to her doing two mornings a week at St Veep's to balance the parish's books. Her many reserves he respected. He was satisfied. He hoped she was.

So here they both were, this Lent-tide, in a place, a special place, a parish with tasks, small and mundane, tiny contributions to the expansion of God's kingdom. Like boot sales, Geoffrey thought, and marched down the aisle towards the vestry door.

'Why boot sales?' his agnostic sister had asked him on one of her brief visits to his patch.

'I don't have a theology of boot sales,' he'd replied with irritation. 'I suppose I feel it brings people together in an area where communities are not always too good at relating, where they are changing too quickly. It releases good energy, gives people who don't have much say, a bit of a say. Celebrates, even. Redistributes the cash, some of it in the Church's direction. Don't you have them at St Veep's?'

'No,' Miss Brighouse had said. 'We have concerts conducted by famous musicians.'

'Each to his own,' Geoffrey had murmured tranquilly. 'I quite like a boot sale myself.'

At the vestry door a different sort of smell greeted him: old boots, newspaper, and a cold dampness inadequately held at bay by Victorian cast-iron heating pipes running round the walls. A slight rustling in the undergrowth of boxes caught his attention as he swung the door closed behind him. Bundles of stuff piled high and stacked round the walls of the small room cast shadows towards him. The brave sunlight of an April morning seeping through a roundel high up in the far wall barely illuminated the space.

'Hello,' Geoffrey called, his tone encouraging as to a dog or child.

There was silence. Geoffrey moved forward towards a pile of men's clothes tastefully surmounted by a bunch of plastic daisies.

'Anyone there?' he called again, and began to push his way through the stacks of stuff. A figure detached itself from behind one of these and made a rush for the door. Geoffrey spun round and clamped a well-timed hand on the stocky figure. In the murky light he discerned an oblong face, with thick black brows and a dark complexion.

'Now what would you be doing here?' he inquired.

For a moment the face said nothing, then the boy shook himself free from Geoffrey's grasp; Geoffrey thought he was going to make a run for it. But he clearly thought better of it.

'I come from my mother,' the boy's accent was south

London with, Geoffrey recognised, Greek overtones. 'She sent me with things for our sale at Easter.'

Geoffrey liked the 'our'. The Kostas family were, he had ascertained, Greek Orthodox, but the mother and grandmother came to St Sylvester's occasionally, probably attracted by the formal ritual which Geoffrey observed in his liturgy. The boys came to the youth club. Whether any of them knew that the Anglican Church was in communion with the Greek Orthodox, whether any of them cared, he had not inquired. The nearest Orthodox church was across the water; not far, he seemed to remember, from St Veep's. As far as Geoffrey was concerned they were in his parish, they had a right to his pastoral care. It was he who had helped break the news of her son's death to Mrs Kostas in Springer's office yesterday, he who had driven her to the hospital and then home. He looked down at this offspring of the Kostas tribe with concern.

'It's Paul, isn't it?'

'No,' said the boy stonily, then added, as an afterthought of politeness, 'Father.'

Geoffrey cursed himself for incompetence. 'Peter?'

The boy nodded. They were, Geoffrey recalled, twins.

'It was kind of your mother to send us things . . .' He thought and then added, 'At this time.'

The boy nodded again. From somewhere outside the building a motor horn sounded with sudden loudness. The boy jumped visibly. 'I'm just going up to the house to have some coffee,' Geoffrey said gently. 'Would you like a cup?'

The boy hesitated, then he said in a sort of wail, 'I can't, I can't. My father says our fortune has left us.'

Then he turned away from Geoffrey and leaned against the pile of coats, crooked his arm across his eyes and wept. The white plastic daisies on top of the pile quivered,

Geoffrey focused his full attention on the stricken boy and started to pray silently. 'Comfort, sustain, repair this Thy child, most merciful Father of all men.' Gradually the boy's shoulders ceased to heave. Geoffrey waited silently. Then he said, 'Come up to the house any time you want to.'

The tears left the boy as quickly as they had overtaken him. He turned towards Geoffrey but his eyes did not take him in. Without a word he made for the door. Geoffrey made no attempt to detain him.

Ten minutes later, Geoffrey pressed the rewind button on the ansaphone in the vicarage hall. The voice was a man's: cultivated, slightly nasal, vaguely familiar. Geoffrey caught the end of the message before identifying its owner. 'So what they're saying is the Kostases' boy's death can't have been an accident. He must have been killed deliberately, murdered in fact.'

'My difficulty,' said Theodora, 'is Mrs Stephanopoulos.'

'My difficulty,' said Geoffrey, 'is Ralph Troutbeck.'

'You go first,' said Theodora courteously, curate to vicar.

'The message on the ansaphone from Troutbeck said the police had had the result of the post-mortem on Paul Kostas and there were signs of bruising on the face and shoulders. The police wanted to know if Troutbeck had noticed these before Kostas disappeared from his class. He said he couldn't remember. The police suspect the boy was hit and then pushed up against the heating unit. Then the electricity was switched on.'

Theodora shuddered.

'I've asked him to come round. He sounded distraught.'

'When?' she asked.

'Now, as soon as he can. I'd be awfully grateful if you could stick around and minister to him a bit. I don't know him very well. I suspect he wants to talk to someone who knows the school but who wasn't part of it. Talking to Springer as his boss might be a bit difficult.' He paused. 'Now tell me about Mrs Stephanopoulos.'

'There are undercurrents,' said Theodora thoughtfully. 'It's not that she's not affected by her daughter's plight, she clearly is. But she's almost fatalistic about it. She blocks off examining lines of inquiry which might lead to Jessica's recovery. It's like playing a game with her. I advance one suggestion and she blocks it, then another and it's blocked again. But all the time I feel that, if I did hit on the right one, she'd own it. But she's not going to come out with it herself.'

'That's a fairly common ploy the guilty make in confession,' said Geoffrey, experienced in such matters. 'They can't face it and bring it out for themselves, but if we can do it for them, they'll acknowledge it.'

'But what could Mrs Stephanopoulos be guilty of?' Theodora inquired.

'Is there anything in the political angle?' Geoffrey pursued. 'Revenge, that sort of thing?'

'They're heavily guarded,' Theodora said. 'There's a guard-chauffeur who doesn't speak much English but has British nationality. According to the account of events Stella had heard, the kidnap car was parked somewhere near his but he apparently didn't notice it. And on the salver in the Stephanopouloses' hall there was this . . .'

The doorbell rang, setting in motion the copper bell on a board at the far end of the kitchen.

'I'll get it,' Geoffrey said, leaping to his feet. 'Could you do us some coffee, if I brought him down here?'

The young man sat at the kitchen table, crouched over the

coffee mug which Theodora had handed him, as though it might be snatched from him. Theodora took in his slim figure, the pale, bony face, long, with the greater part given over to forehead, dark eyes recessed under dark eyebrows, a short nose and a mouth which pouted, the underlip thrust out and suggesting self-pity. His hair, of which there was a great deal, was dark and curly, worn long. It cascaded down over his neck and collar. It looked, Theodora thought, like a wig. She noticed long, beautiful hands, strong and white like a pianist's. Was he nervous, she wondered, or only acting nervousness? Was he disguising real nervousness by acting nervous. His bodily movement seemed too considered. Of course he was a drama specialist. It probably left him without much spontaneity. She thought of the other Troutbeck she knew. Apart from the dark good looks, they had nothing particularly to relate them. He was dressed in fawn cords and a darker, soft fawn pullover. The predominant image was one of softness.

Geoffrey allowed him to talk, letting him repeat his story, prompting, encouraging, engaging with him. Theodora was moved to professional admiration of Geoffrey's technique, all the more because it did not advertise itself as a technique. Still, it didn't seem to be working. Ralph Troutbeck was no more relaxed now than he had been twenty minutes ago when he first came. His knuckles showed white as he clasped the mug.

'So how did you describe what happened to the police?' Geoffrey asked, to allow him to give a slightly different angle to his narrative.

'I told them,' Troutbeck answered – was his tone defiant? Theodora wondered – 'I told them that I took the group for fourth section, first after break.' He licked his lips.

'Not the easiest time,' Theodora murmured to help him.

He glanced up at her almost for the first time. Her fellow teacher's remark seemed to reassure him.

'Right,' he said making the monosyllable a triphthong. 'They tend to develop their own interests over break and it's difficult to settle them. As I said, it's a big group. I honestly can't see how one person can be expected to keep tabs on forty fourth years – year tens,' he emended, correcting his pre-National Curriculum phraseology.

'Forty does seem a bit large,' Theodora soothed him again.

'Muriel's away. My colleague. I had her lot as well as my usual ones. Hence the two Kostases. They split them into different classes because they were such a pain together.'

'How a pain?'

'Oh, well, I suppose they're just terribly good at causing trouble, starting things off. They're into things military. I suppose it's a tough culture. Cyprus and all that. What I'm saying is, I suppose, they carry weight in their group. They're bullies, if you like. If they aren't on your side you won't even get the attention of the rest of the kids because they're all busy listening to the relevant Kostas.'

Troutbeck stopped and looked embarrassed. Theodora reflected that teachers are trained nowadays to suppose that if they can't control a class, it's their fault, not the class's. In Theodora's experience that was not always true. Some classes set out to destroy teachers and did so. Had that happened to Troutbeck, she wondered. Had there been a row? Had things got out of hand, groups splitting off and just ignoring instructions, going about their own unruly business, from angels to devils, from pupils to opponents in twenty minutes? Had conversations turned to laughter, jeering and calling out? Had Ralph moved from exasperation to panic? Had he lost his grip, his nerve,

and finally his temper, and had the result of that been a
boy thrown against an electric bar and killed? It was such
a silly and unlikely death, the sort of death which comes
from someone panicking. It occurred to Theodora to
wonder what someone like Troutbeck was doing at SWL.
Was he serving his time before he could move on to higher,
more congenial things? Why wasn't he writing his play
or his novel, oozing into journalism, advertising or TV?
Theodora brought her attention back to Troutbeck's tone.
It had a hint of hysteria, compelled, forced into reason and
control, she thought.

'You took them from their classroom to the hall?'
Geoffrey asked.

'Yes. Their two classrooms are next door to each other
on level three.'

Geoffrey remembered how the levels of the bleak building seemed identical to him, and wondered whether they
had any distinguishing marks to someone who worked in it.

'The Councillor Ferrin Hall leads off the end of the
corridor. 'It's three classrooms put together, really, but it's
big enough for drama,' Troutbeck continued.

'Where's the closed classroom, the one not in use?'

'It's next to the hall.'

'They'd pass it on their way to the hall then?'

'Right.'

'Are you sure all the pupils made it from their classrooms
to the hall?'

Troutbeck hesitated.

'Did you take a register?' Geoffrey pressed.

Troutbeck flushed, 'Of course. But . . .'

Theodora prompted him. 'The Kostas boys looked alike.'

Troutbeck glanced at her again with relief and nodded.
'It's really not possible to check there's a face behind every

voice that answers,' he said hopelessly. 'If you did, you'd never start the lesson.'

'Do you think it might have been possible for one of the Kostases – Paul – to duck into the closed classroom?'

'I suppose so.'

'And then?'

'I told you the rest. It was near the end of the lesson. I'd decided to let them go a bit early. They were milling around by the door. I heard a girl scream. At first I couldn't locate it. Then I dashed out and went next door.' He stopped and swallowed. 'He was hanging over the electric unit, all twisted. He was sort of wrapped round it. Apparently it was part of the new central heating plant.At the time I didn't realise how he'd died. In fact I wasn't sure he was dead.'

There was a pause before Geoffrey asked, 'What did you do?'

'I came out, shut the door, and dispatched a couple of the more dependable types: one to the office to ring for an ambulance, and one to get Springer.'

'What did he say?'

'He said . . . his first words were, "It's going to be very hard to support you on a professional basis on this one, Ralph. At the bottom line, when the chips are down, we teachers, that is you, Ralph, have to carry the can. I know you won't feel too comfortable with that, Ralph, but we both know that's how it is." '

Troutbeck had quite a good imitation of his head-teacher's voice, Geoffrey noticed. He'd caught the equivocal vowels, half mid-atlantic manager, half south London bloke, quite accurately.

'But you can't be blamed for a pupil's accidental death.'

'Springer seems quite content that I should be. It's certainly the end of my teaching career.' Ralph's tone was not, Theodora thought, particularly anguished; there was, indeed, almost satisfaction in it. Was he masochistic or just genuinely relieved that he could now give up, even dishonourably, a job for which he had no talent.

'But even if you have to bear some responsibility for the control of the class, that's a different matter from saying that you actually killed the boy.' Geoffrey had the air of tidying up the topic in a way which would have suited his previous role as a naval officer rather more than his present one of sympathetic pastor. 'What is it that the police are saying? I wasn't too clear from your message on the ansaphone.'

Troutbeck took his time. Then he said, 'The police had me and Springer in together and told us that they were treating the death as an intentional killing, not an accident. They feel the medical evidence shows that the boy was in some sort of a fight, and that he was deliberately thrown and held on to the electric unit.'

'Wouldn't anyone who held the boy on to the unit also have been electrocuted?' Theodora realised she had become so interested in the details of the method she too had abandoned the pastoral voice.

'If he was hurled against the unit, no one need have held him. But if he was held, whoever held him would have had to have been insulated in some way. Perhaps by wearing those heavy rubber gloves that electricians use when dealing with power lines. There's plenty of spare workmen's clobber lying around.'

Theodora shuddered at the thought of such premeditation.

'What about his fellow pupils?' Geoffrey asked. 'Could any of them have done it?'

'The police say they all give each other alibis.'

'But don't they also give you an alibi? You couldn't have been out of sight of them when you were teaching them.'

Troutbeck flushed. 'I was out of their sight just once. I had to go back to the classroom for some more copies of the script we were working on. I was only away for five minutes and they had work set.' He was defensive. 'It was early in the class. I'm pretty certain the Kostases were both with me at that point.'

'Both?' Geoffrey pressed.

'Well, one certainly was, because he was near the door as I returned.'

'Which one?' Geoffrey pressed.

Ralph practically wept. 'I don't know, they both look alike to me.'

'Have the police any ideas? If he wasn't killed by accident or by one of his fellow pupils in a fight, who could have killed him? And why?'

'Well, it wasn't me,' said Troutbeck with vehemence. 'I can't say I liked the Kostas boys, or indeed any of that appalling year, but I didn't kill anyone. I reckon the pol-ice'd do better going over some of those thugs that his family seem related to.'

'You know his family then?' Theodora pressed the question.

'Not especially. But I've seen some of them picking the boys up at the gate after school sometimes. I always assume the Greeks run the same sort of mafia as the Italians.' Troutbeck was almost dismissive. 'They all seem to have a fair amount of cash about them, and I don't think it comes from running Greek restaurants.'

'What do this particular bit of the Kostas clan do for a living?' Theodora inquired.

'The father's got a transport business. HGVs and vans and things.'

'Have you . . .' Theodora was tentative. 'Have you felt able to meet the family yet?'

Troutbeck shook his head. 'I wanted to. I did try when Mrs Kostas came up to the school after . . .' He broke off. 'Springer wouldn't let me. He said it would be better not.'

'I know it will be difficult, but I think you should.'

'I tried to say a word to the brother, the other twin.' Troutbeck stopped.

'What happened?'

'He spat at me,' Troutbeck brought out. 'Then he said his father would want payment.'

Geoffrey was startled. 'Money?'

'Oh no,' Troutbeck said, and was the hint of triumph, Theodora wondered again, masochism or relief? 'I think it's my blood they'll want.'

When Troutbeck had gone, Geoffrey paced up and down the kitchen as if it were quarterdeck. 'Two problems then. One, who killed Kostas and why; and two, how can we help Troutbeck?'

'Do I take it that you don't think Troutbeck killed Kostas?'

Geoffrey ruminated. 'I don't think it's impossible. I'd say he was something of an hysteric, wouldn't you?'

Theodora nodded. 'But we're not, you know, police. Surely we would agree that our – I mean the Church's – duties are the same whoever did it. The Kostas family and Troutbeck have an equal right to our concern.'

Why did Theodora sound so anxious, Geoffrey wondered. He was in full agreement with her. 'We've rather left to one side,' he said in his best vicar's manner, 'your problem with Mrs Stephanopoulos and her daughter's kidnap.'

'Not entirely,' Theodora was thoughtful.

'Surely unconnected.'

'I expect you're right,' Theodora agreed. But she did wonder. She was sure she was not mistaken. She had certainly seen the Kostas car hire firm's card on the table beneath the statue of the Virgin and child at the Stephanopouloses' house, which was odd when you considered they seem to have gone everywhere by embassy transport and the Kostas firm was on the other side of the water.

CHAPTER SIX

Artistic Life

'An icon is a diagram of essential, eternal truths.' Cromwell tossed his black mane from his broad brow. The Hapgood twins crossed their legs in unison, leaned back in their chairs and gave themselves up to the appreciation of an accomplished performer. Eulalia Topglass, from one of the southern states of North America, wrote Cromwell's comment in her notebook with the bitten end of a pencil. The Canon of Exeter's niece, Candida Warren, reserved her judgement. She reckoned she knew about ecclesiastical art and distrusted actors. In the back row, Clarissa Bennet, the fair-haired girl whose eye had met Theodora's in the hall, staring over the banisters yesterday, spread her fingers out in front of her and concentrated on their essential diagrammatic form.

On the screen hung at one end of the large studio at the top of St Veep's main school were projected side by side two slides. The one on Cromwell's right hand was of a conventional 1930s portrait of a middle-class English woman, shown three-quarter length standing beside a window and turned partly towards the garden depicted in the background. The one on the other side of him presented to the audience a likeness, in the muted blue and silver of Greek fourteenth-century icons, of the Virgin and child.

'What strikes us first about an icon is how much is missing,' Cromwell went on. 'The nearest parallel in literature is Greek classical drama. There, all that the nineteenth century taught us to look for – the glorification of the unique individual, the psychological nuances which divide us from each other and make us unrepeatedly peculiar – are absent.'

Cromwell's pointer tapped the Virgin and child. The dark eyes of the Virgin, who looked neither young nor old, gazed out to meet those of the audience. Theodora looked at its lines. She'd seen it before, she realised, recently. Then, with a sweeping movement, he flipped the pointer in the air and caught it in his other hand and tapped the picture on his right.

Eulalia, who was concentrating hard, jumped. The pointer circled the second picture. Helena Braithwaite, as pictured by Phillip de Laslo © 1930, became the focus of fifty pairs of eyes. Like the Virgin, Lady Helena was in blue, the sleeves of her dress lined with white. Theodora had the unsettling experience of gazing at her grandmother's familiar face, forty years younger than she had known it. The Hapgood twins leaned forward to study the costume more closely. Was she wearing a tea-gown, they wondered? They had heard of such things in the literature of the period. Stylistic detail was their speciality, and they were eager to learn. In one hand Lady Helena had a rose, the other rested on the back of a drawing-room chair. The face turned towards the window and looking out on to the garden was vivacious, eager, not quite smiling, as though about to greet pleasant visitors. The garden in the background showed an herbaceous border in its late summer glory.

'Compare and contrast,' said Cromwell. 'What, instinctively, is the reaction to which the artist compels us here?'

The question was rhetorical. But Eulalia, more used to the participatory methods of American education, responded. 'We look for the story?'

'Go on.'

'Why the dress, the view, the expression on the face?'

'Just so. Even the symbols – the rose, the garden – which might lure us to the universal, are here made idiosyncratic, particular to this woman in this setting at this time. We do not have a diagram, we have history. Commonplace history.'

'But that's not fair,' Candida Warren burst out. 'No one is asking us to worship Lady Braithwaite.'

'I sure find her a really attractive lady,' said Eulalia courteously, defending her own type.

The Hapgoods grinned their approval. The delight of Cromwell's session, they had agreed, was the scope it allowed for both universal type and individual character to emerge. Theodora, in the back row, found herself similarly happy to be where the discussion of ideas was natural and valued; where, in fact, education was taking place. She had come to hear Cromwell, taking advantage of the pleasant convention of the establishment which allowed staff to attend each other's sixth-form classes. Theodora had been surprised and flattered to be asked by Doris King if she might look in on Theodora's class on St John with her Oxbridge pair. 'I've often felt the author of the gospel was less Greek and more Hebrew than Doctor Dodd supposes, and I'd like to hear the arguments.' Theodora, in return, had courteously wondered if she might attend Miss King's session on Alcestis with her lower-sixth group. 'I've long felt we were meant to find an element of parody of male querulousness in Admetus and I'd like to hear the arguments.' Both had come together with other colleagues to hear Cromwell's 'Art for Amateurs' course, a fixture for Tuesday afternoon in the Lent term sixth-form calendar, and hugely popular. To Theodora too it had offered a welcome release from worry about Jessica.

Theodora gazed at the two pictures displayed on either side of the art master. The long white studio with its glass roof and northern light produced a contemplative religious atmosphere. The electricity had not, on Cromwell's order, been switched on, so the two slides showed up sharp and clear.

She reflected on what Cromwell had said. Of course icons had a different use from mere portraits, in which there must always be an element of self-glorification. Icons are part of a living faith and its practices, part of a ritual which could help to bring people into God's presence. They are a mechanism, a device for changing us by the discipline of prayer and meditation. There are limits on what one could do with and by an icon. It is not possible, for example, to hang it on the wall of a gallery beside Lady Braithwaite's portrait. Icons aren't really pictures at all, Theodora thought. They're things, holy things, like churches or crosses or altars.

'The icon,' Cromwell was pressing on, 'resembles certain seventeenth-century Dutch paintings, for example flower paintings, where every bloom has a particular symbolism in terms of human virtue. Such paintings intend to tell us something like a puzzle. They do not invite, they do not require us to use our imagination. Lady Braithwaite's portrait may tell us about love, a particular emotion; the icon appeals not to love but to worship in the universal mode.'

Candida Warren stirred uncomfortably. This was all rather far from her uncle's sound Anglican tradition.

Cromwell glared round as if scenting reservations on the part of his audience. 'It is a sign of the degeneration of our times that we are incapable of making that sort of distinction, or of recognising the true and different natures of things which only superficially resemble each other. To us all paintings are just paintings. Are we not diminished by that failure in discrimination? In the past, icons were objects of power, not artifice. Hence the iconoclasts of the Byzantine period supposed they were destroying pernicious and potent things, not decorations and superfluities. Icons to the iconoclast possessed demonic power.'

Candida felt she must put in a word for Anglican sanity here. 'But it's we who give them the power,' she burst out. 'Of themselves they are nothing – just wood and gilt. And whatever *we* give power to is just an idol.'

Cromwell swung round to her. 'Never underestimate the power of symbols. Advertisers don't. Politicians don't. In the past people killed for the possession of them.' At that moment there was a crash. Clarissa Bennet fell forward with a sort of sigh. The Hapgood twins, who were sitting to the right of her, turned their concerned profiles in her direction. Cromwell ceased in mid-flow. 'What's up?'

The more flippant element chorused, 'Lights, lights! There was much scraping of chairs and solicitous inquiry. Clarissa was aided from the room by Miss King and Eulalia. Cromwell simply stood with his hands folded over his pointer, leaning on it like a shepherd on his crook, waiting for the hubbub to die down. Theodora scrutinised the tall figure of the man. He was quite egoist enough for his only perceptible emotion to be impatience at the interruption of his discourse. She recalled Clarissa's small body bent forward, her eyes pinned on to his face, just prior to the faint. One might suppose Clarissa had been very interested indeed in what Cromwell was saying.

'What sort of a child was Jessica?' Theodora inquired later that afternoon in the staff common room.

'Not, I would have said, too happy here,' Miss Brighouse answered her. 'She came, of course, late. I mean she didn't come at twelve. Latecomers sometimes take a while to settle in. Of course, she'd travelled a lot and that's both an advantage and a disadvantage here. Socially she fitted in perfectly well. Her mama was here, of course.'

'Academically,' Miss King put her oar in, 'she wasn't quite up to our first-division standards. Gaps in all subjects. The sciences particularly. A familiarity with the subway systems of New York and Istanbul are no substitute for basic physics.'

'What was she good at?' Theodora pursued.

'Art,' said Oenone Troutbeck, raising her head from packing her briefcase. 'She was one of Cromwell's coterie.'

'Not religion?' Theodora asked, remembering the cross and Mrs Stephanopoulos's remarks. There was a silence.

'Not widely popular as a subject area. Mr Mere, how shall I put it, has a certain dampening effect on his pupils.'

'As a partly Anglican foundation . . .' Theodora ventured.

'Chaplains have always found us a difficult furrow to plough,' said Miss Brighouse with satisfaction. 'Not an easy role for a man, I mean, relating positively to clever adolescent girls.'

'They tend to run rings round them.' Oenone was blunter.

'The last one who tried it here had a nervous breakdown within the year. The religious position, when argued for in rational terms, tends to sound a little simplistic. Wouldn't you say?' Oenone turned towards Theodora.

'I agree it's better to live it than to argue it.' Theodora felt constrained to say. She was beginning to feel that too much of Oenone might be rather tiresome. 'Who were Jessica's friends?' She brought the conversation back to her line of exploration.

'She didn't seem to have anyone very close,' Miss King answered. 'There was an aquaintance with the Bennet girl. I suppose the connection was Cromwell and the art club.'

The clock chimed in the distance. There was a flurry of wrists checking watches. Briefcases were hauled on to tables; not a plastic bag in sight, Theodora noticed. The two mathematicians seized violin cases and made for the hall. Ieuan Colt embraced the double bass in its corner and propelled it in front of him across the parquet as if it were a recalcitrant dancing partner. There was a general air of end of day and beginning of evening, an almost visible assumption of different attitudes and pursuits. Education did not finish, it simply changed gear.

Theodora piled her books together, hesitated a moment, and then set off down the hall across the marble towards the sixth-form wing. Before she reached it, she turned left to the medical room. The room was dimly lit and smelt of disinfectant. It was small and sparsely furnished. It was also cold. Illness was not encouraged at St Veep's. You were not supposed to be sick during school hours; there were more important things to do. At the far end of the room there was a medical couch.

Theodora approached cautiously. 'How are you feeling now?'

The girl snapped her eyes open suddenly. 'I'm much better, thank you,' Clarissa paused. 'It was the heat you know. Those top rooms are terribly stuffy. We all breath in each other's air.'

Theodora nodded. She wasn't sure whether she believed Clarissa or not. She looked at the barely visible contours of the triangular face with its tongues of fair hair framing it. 'I wondered, I believe you were a friend . . . you knew Jessica Stephanopoulos.'

There was no eye-contact. Clarissa ran the back of her hand across her brow. 'I wonder, do you think I could possibly have some more cold water?'

Theodora looked round for a glass. She realised she was going to be made to pay for any information she obtained. 'It's important we get some sort of notion of who she knew, who her contacts were.'

'Why?' Clarissa asked.

It was a fair question but also, Theodora felt, slightly manipulative, Truth would be the only rock, any manoeuvring with such a one would only result in shipwreck.

'My own intuition is she had some sort of premonition, or fear that something was going to happen to her, and she may have shared that feeling with someone close, a friend, perhaps here.'

'Why me? I'm not in her year.'

'You were both members of the art club, Mr Cromwell's club.'

Clarissa did not deny it. She sipped her cold water and then turned on her side, cradling her fair head on her hand. The chaise-longue effect was almost of someone enjoying valetudinarianism, Elizabeth Barrett Browning.

Clarissa looked at Theodora consideringly. 'Lady Braithwaite was your grandmother?'

Theodora nodded.

'My grandmother was here too, and both my aunts.'

Theodora took her meaning at once. 'That's just what I mean. It's a network, isn't it? And over three generations now. That can't be too common. If someone was rather insecure – frightened perhaps – within the family setting, it would be easy, sensible almost, to make this institution the place to put your trust in.'

Clarissa nodded. 'I think it's rather a new thing for us, I mean for women to be able to do. My brother, Roderick, he's ten years older than me. He takes it as a matter of course that he'll be able to call up all sorts of help from people he was at school with. I suppose we're just about beginning to be able to do the same thing.' She stopped short, as though drawn too much along a path she had not intended to tread.

'Was Jessica in need of a network?' Theodora's question was quietly put but Clarissa, she thought, looked wary.

'People group by interest here rather than age. Or background. We're very democratic.'

Theodora hid a smile. The intellectual sophistication outran, she felt, the social. 'So what were Jessica's connections?'

'Well, Cromwell's coterie was certainly her milieu. She'd seen an awful lot, you know.' There was a spark almost of animation, almost of envy in Clarissa's tone. 'She'd seen the galleries in most of Europe and she'd been to MOMA in New York.'

'So she had some standing in Cromwell's coterie?'

'I suppose you could put it like that.'

'Was she interested in any particular sort of art?'

Clarissa considered. Then she gave Theodora the benefit of her rare level eye-contact. 'Have you considered the possibility of religious art?' she said slowly.

For some reason which Theodora could not at all analyse, she suddenly felt like shivering. 'What do you mean?'

'I think Jessica would have appreciated the icon. I mean she was religious. Cromwell was right, you know. Icons aren't pictures at all, they are part of religion. Like a rosary or a talisman.'

Theodora did not consider talismen religious, but she knew what Clarissa was trying to say. She wasn't sure whether she was amused or irritated by the girl's didacticism.

'Do you happen to know where the icon Mr Cromwell showed us this afternoon was from?'

'I imagine it's a slide of something' – she paused as if uncertain – 'known to Mr Cromwell. I'm afraid I can't help you over its provenance.'

'Was Jessica friendly with anyone else? Mr Mere, for example?'

'Oh him. Well she was going to be confirmed, so I suppose she did know him. He certainly likes distinguished families.'

Theodora got up. 'You've been very helpful,' she said, gazing down at Clarissa.

'Surely not,' replied the latter faintly as she reclined further back on her couch.

CHAPTER SEVEN

Night School

Geoffrey thought how very pleasant the school was when there were no pupils in it. By five minutes past four, the building of SWL comprehensive school was deserted by staff and pupils alike. By four-fifteen the boilers had been switched off and the smell of cleaning fluid replaced that of coke. By seven-fifteen the school had entered its evening role. From somewhere in the area of the hall came the sound of taped music and the high, jolly voices emanating from the women's aerobic class. A clutch of Open University philosophers chatted with nervous confidence as they rearranged desks in one of the bleak classrooms. A vacuum cleaner droned a couple of landings away. There was a purposefulness, indeed a good temper, pervading the building, which was missing from Geoffrey's experience of the place in its daytime incarnation.

Geoffrey had left the Lambretta at home and sprinted the half-mile to the school. He bounded up the stairs. He was beginning to be able to find his way to the head's office without getting lost. He'd once asked McGrath why the head's office was three floors up and unlabelled. 'Gives stroppy parents time to cool off before they can get their hands on him,' had been McGrath's answer.

Springer had called the meeting for seven-thirty. Geoffrey, a punctual man, was surprised to see others there before him. Cherry, the second deputy, sat very upright in her denim boiler suit, next to Springer's desk. Ralph Troutbeck crouched in the foetal position on a sagging easy chair opposite her. Just inside the door was McGrath, not yet sitting down and looking, in service fashion, as though he didn't expect to be invited to do so and would be perfectly happy to stand for the next two hours.

'Yah, yah, Ok, I hear you,' Springer was mouthing into the phone. Geoffrey noticed that a mobile one with a space-age extending aerial had replaced the old corded one. It seemed, however, that Springer had not yet got the idea that the instrument could be used away from his desk. Or else perhaps, Geoffrey thought, he felt his desk was base. He waved to Geoffrey with his free hand. It wasn't a bad imitation of the powerful executive greeting junior staff. Geoffrey unslung a chair from the stack in the corner, and placed it opposite McGrath and next to Cherry. Springer finished barking into the phone, spoilt the impression of smart office modernity by getting the aerial tangled up in the flex of his desk light, and turned towards Geoffrey.

'I got your memo re. your Miss B. joining us. That's fine by me. We'll need someone to take notes.'

Geoffrey admired Springer's thriftiness. He'd wanted Theodora to come along because he was going to ask her to do something about getting the Kostas family and Ralph Troutbeck to speak to each other. She'd need to be drawn in if that was to be done in the near future.

Theodora, arriving three minutes later, found a group

clearly not at ease with itself. She all but sniffed the atmosphere. She scented the irreconcilable. She was an old hand.

Springer consulted his digital watch which told him the
time in New York and Canberra and called them to order.
'I guess it's time we made a start, folks.' He turned to
Theodora whom he had never met before. 'Welcome
aboard, Theo. This is Cherry, my first deputy. And Jim,
sorry Mike, McGrath, our man in the boiler room. What's
your official title Jim, er, Mike? I always forget it.' He
didn't, however, wait for an answer. 'And Ralph there,' he
went on with rapid distaste, 'I think you know.'

Cherry smiled her warm social services smile, McGrath
gave her a neck bow, and Ralph made no sign that he had
heard any of this.

Springer took up his favourite position half crouching,
half sitting on the front of his desk. It put his head just a
little above anyone else's in the room, but left his feet
dangling six inches from the floor. 'First of all, I'd like to
thank you all very warmly indeed and very sincerely for
giving up your time and agreeing to come along this
evening.'

Theodora wondered if he had made the annual parent-
governor meeting his model for this get-together. She
imagined you might have to be especially grateful to any
parents who managed to tear themselves away from the
telly to come to one of those in an area like this.

'What we need to do, what we absolutely *must* do first,'
Springer was getting into his stride, 'is to set our parameters. Which are, of course, I hasten to say, negotiable.'
He showed no sign of stopping to negotiate. 'I can't think
of any better way of doing this than being one hundred
per cent open with you and just sharing my thinking with
you. Off the top of my head.' He gave a portion of

eye-contact to each member of the group in turn, to assure himself that they'd managed to follow him this far.

'As you know, our numbers will drop if we don't recruit. Money follows pupils. We can't afford, we just can't afford – ' he looked round sternly – 'to scare our clients off in this way.'

Theodora could scarcely believe her ears. Was the man mad? Could he really be talking about the death, the possible murder of one of his pupils?

'The governors,' he went on, 'had an urgent meeting this afternoon. They're very worried, very worried indeed, I can tell you, and rightly so in my opinion, about the school's reputation. Nothing scares parents away more than . . .' Theodora waited. Surely he couldn't be at a loss for words? 'Than something like this.' He shot a venomous glance at Ralph. 'In matters like this, parental perceptions are all-important.'

Theodora wasn't sure whether his attitude was risible or macabre.

'I want it cleared up pronto, tout de suite. Do you follow me? I'd like us to be all absolutely together, shoulder to shoulder, on this one.'

Theodora decided there was nothing she could do except relax and simply collect the jumble of dissonant attitudes. She glanced across at Geoffrey. He remained impassive. His eye was fixed on a distant part of the ceiling above Springer's head. She reflected that he knew Springer of old, so perhaps he was inured to his moral oafishness.

'What I'm urging us all to do, what we absolutely must do is,' he leaned towards them from his elevated position, 'be totally, one hundred per cent frank with the police. No point in hiding anything. For good or ill.' He glanced again at Ralph who remained comatose, his head sunk in his chest, his arms tightly folded. 'For good or ill,' he repeated, and then surged on.

'I made it perfectly obvious when I saw their top man, their inspector, that he could rely on me, on us all, one hundred per cent. The police investigation, if you can call it that – I wasn't over-impressed by their methods – makes it absolutely plain, plain as a pikestaff, that it must have been an inside job. It must have been somebody in the know. D'you follow me? Now I'm not pointing the finger at anyone.' He flung a glance at Ralph. 'Anyone can make a mistake. But what we must do – you, me, absolutely everybody concerned – we've got to put our heads together and come clean over this one. For the good of the school.'

He paused. He appeared to have come to an end. His audience stirred uncomfortably.

'Hang on a mo, Lance.' Cherry turned her serious face to her team manager. 'Do we need to do some criminal profiling here? Bronfenbrenner and Bronfenbrenner's work in the States in the eighties has some really, really interesting things to say about criminal stereotyping in detection. I mean, how helpful is it to say it's an inside job? I think we need to be very clear on this one. Are you saying one of us deliberately killed Paul Kostas?'

The uttering of the boy's name seemed suddenly to strip away the mass of verbiage in which Springer had clad the event. Before he could answer, Ralph Troutbeck uncoiled from his foetal position and ran his hands through his web of hair.

'I've had enough of this.' He leaned forward towards Springer. 'Stop pointing the finger at me.'

'No one's pointing any fingers, Ralph.'

'Pointing the finger at me,' he went on relentlessly. His tone was slurred. Theodora, sitting next to him, felt him sway slightly. She judged him to be just about drunk.

'Well, we have to face it, Ralph, you didn't control your class. Your parameters.'

Theodora could feel Springer's panic. It was being changed into violence and bullying even as he spoke.

'*Blast* my parameters. No one,' Troutbeck glared round, 'no one could control that set of morons. That doesn't mean I killed any of them.'

'But Ralph,' Cherry was all sweet reasonableness, 'you weren't exactly in a positive relationship with the Kostas twins.'

Ralph swung round. Theodora noticed that drink made a cliché of his actions as well of his words and tone. He began to stab the air with his forefinger like a B-film actor miming drunkenness. 'No one, no one at all had a "positive relationship", as you so preposterously call it – where do you get your jargon from, dearie? – with the Kostases. They were accomplished little bullies together and ruffians separately. They ran the fourth-year mafia quite as brutally as their dad runs the Cypriot mafia from his transport HQ. I might point out he's just done six months for GBH on one of his neighbours. His boys were just following in Dad's footsteps. And if it comes to "negative relationships" ' – Ralph turned his blood-shot eyes on Springer – 'you know damn well you came near to excluding them last term.'

Cherry, always glad to improve a bad situation, smiled happily at Springer. 'That's right, Lance. There was that business with the knife.'

Springer flushed all over his pale, team-manager's face. 'That was a joint decision of the governing body. They have the final say. I was perfectly happy to accept their verdict. Perfectly happy, I said so at the time. I had it minuted. It's in the minutes. We're professionals. We've got to live with that. That's what we've got to live with.'

McGrath, who had in the end decided to sit down, folded his arms over his chest and gazed at the warring factions. 'If we're looking for people who didn't like or were downright scared of the Kostas twins, we'll be here all night. They were tough little bleeders. The point is, who had the opportunity to kill one of them? We'd do better sticking to that.'

'Well, Mike, I guess you'd have to be on that list, wouldn't you?' said Cherry. She might have been offering him a box of chocolates. 'I seem to remember you were in the utility room at the end of the corridor about that time.'

McGrath was more composed than his superiors. 'Yes,' he said equably. 'I was fixing broken chairs in the utility room. As I told the police. I was there from the beginning of break at ten forty-five, to the middle of the third lesson, eleven-twenty, when Kostas was killed.'

'Did you hear anything?' Geoffrey inquired, relinquishing his eye-contact with the ceiling and turning to McGrath.

The latter shook his head. 'I'd plenty to do. These kids don't just break furniture, they wreck it. I was hammering. There's always a fair amount of noise from the school. There were drills going from the builders outside. It's not what you might call – ' he glanced at Springer – 'a quiet working environment.'

Springer suddenly snapped. 'It's a perfectly OK environment. There's absolutely nothing wrong with it. We've identified a lot of problems in that area over the last three years and we've met those problems, surmounted those challenges . . .' His voice trailed off as though he could find no comfort in his own words any more. He sounded almost tearful.

Theodora eyed him. He looked to her like someone who took refuge in jargon in order not to have to think.

Language was a substitute reality for Springer. You didn't have to mean anything by it, it didn't point to anything beyond itself. Hence he'd 'address problems' and 'identify solutions' rather than look reality in the face. But when real life burst in and would not be denied – as in the murder of one of his pupils – he could not find the language to evade that reality. Theodora wondered what he thought education was for, if not to provide the vocabulary appropriate to the event.

'I wonder,' she began tentatively, 'if it would help to be certain what each of us was doing at the time of the boy's death.' Her eye swept over Cherry and Springer, Ralph and McGrath. 'We do want, don't we, to find out what happened and who is responsible for this death?'

There was a sudden flash outside the windows, and the lights went out. There was a moment's absolute silence, then a sound of doors banging and a hubbub from below.

'What the hell . . .?' said Springer.

'These electricians certainly don't seem too lucky,' said Cherry.

'Set of clowns,' McGrath moved towards the door. 'I've got some spare lighting gear in the utility room.'

'I'll give you a hand.' Geoffrey leapt to his feet to follow him out. They moved cautiously down the darkened corridor, lit now only by the faraway and often reflected lights from the main road.

The ladies' aerobics class could be heard joining the Open University philosophers two storeys below.

'I'll have to get some lights to them. They're both keen groups. They'll want to go on. And of course they pay for the hire nowadays.' McGrath manipulated the key bunch on his belt. 'If you'd like to take these back to Mr Springer, sir, I'll get some of this stuff downstairs.' He handed

Geoffrey a couple of standing lamps and indicated some more complicated apparatus at the back of his lobby. He seemed to know what he was doing.

It struck Geoffrey they were really rather well equipped to deal with the emergency. Had they perhaps had to cope with this sort of thing often during the rewiring?

Geoffrey seized the standing lamps and turned to go back down the corridor. As he did so his eye was caught by a pair of gloves wedged into the pipes which ran at shoulder height round one side of the tiny room. They were large and heavy and made of rubber. Geoffrey had seen their like before: they were the sort of insulated gloves that electricians sometimes had occasion to wear in the workshops of aircraft carriers.

Theodora had refused Geoffrey's offer to accompany her home. He'd wanted to look in on the youth club down in the old drill hall next to the primary school. There was no point in hanging about. The sudden plunge into darkness had made further discussion impossible as far as the members of Lance Springer's meeting were concerned. The atmosphere was heavy with suspicion, as dense as the smell from the sewage works which swept down the river when the wind was in the west. But there was nothing, as far as she could see, that she could do about it.

'How about supper, ten-fifteen?' Geoffrey had flung over his shoulder before he'd sprinted off. It was eight-forty. She had time to walk back to the vicarage.

She set off through the parish, down the long high street. At this end the tall Edwardian houses had basements and steep steps up to front doors, where panels of a dozen names beside as many bells suggested full occupation of the premises. The skips parked permanently in the front gardens overflowed with interesting materials and functioned, Theodora knew, as a sort of informal swap-shop: a nice bit of hardboard would go out and a couple of discarded chairs would go in. It struck her as an admirable system.

Further down the street, the solid detached houses gave way to earlier, more decayed Victorian terraces of shops. Many of these were still open. They were family businesses, and closed only when their owners went to bed. Entering them was like entering someone's front room. The smell of un-English food drifted out from back kitchens. Dark-skinned Asian children played games on the shop floor, clamouring in unknown tongues. The chippy was Chinese. Only the Prince of Orange was in indigenous hands, run with even-handed brutality by an ex-SAS man and his lady.

Theodora loved it deeply. It had been part of her apprenticeship in learning how to live in this unfamiliar society to find out who counted, who could do what, what the networks were. 'Map your culture,' her pastoral studies tutor at theological college had advised. And she had. She had observed, reflected, prayed and chosen her priorities.

The youth club was mainly boys, so she left that to Geoffrey. The old people's coven was mainly women, so she took it on. They tossed each other for the hospital and Geoffrey won, so she took the prison. It introduced her to the female network which was different from the male. It was the wives and mothers who suffered when the men had no work or went to prison – though sometimes their incarceration was a relief. Once they knew and trusted her, the wives, sisters and daughters asked the small favours of the postman from her. There was no quantifiable reward in this. These people were not Christian worshippers. They would not come to church, seek instruction or enter the

Christian life. But she knew that both she and Geoffrey were increasingly acceptable in a large number of households. They were seen as part of what English society had to offer: like compulsory schooling and free health care, they were taken for part of the deal. Indeed, since they lived and dressed differently from other people, because they were clearly in their daily habits religious, they were more easily understood and accepted by the immigrant population than other public bodies like the social services, whose ministrations were seen as intrusive.

Where, Theodora wondered, as she tramped past the video shops and the pornography parlours, where in this mixed brew had the Kostas boy's death come from? She circled the patch and learned it street by street, shop by shop, family by family, assimilating it as best she could. The houses were easy. But the tower blocks which loomed behind them were intractable. Traffic swirled about them, cutting them off from casual pedestrian access. Getting to one was like planning a campaign. Their ugliness seemed to kill ordinary human affections. It was in one of these, Theodora knew, that the Kostas family lived. The tower blocks were what had replaced the terraces which bombs of the Second World War had destroyed. The area had flourished between the wars and until the fifties. Then the indigenous population had grown richer. In the sixties and seventies the sons and daughters had moved out to Sidcup, leaving behind the old, the feckless, or the miserably unfortunate. Then the immigrant population had flowed in and created a new life.

It wasn't peaceful. Energy, on some nights and in some areas, could become explosive. Theodora was surprised to find how like Africa it was; how climate played a part in the eruption of violence. Hot nights brought it on; rain stopped play. Violence started with noise, ear splitting as a pub door swung open; then there would be the sound of breaking glass, women screaming, an explosion of motorbikes or car engines racing, then the pounding of feet. Someone would start running, others joined in; it was impossible to tell whether it was a race or a hunt. Were they running from something or towards it? Sometimes, it seemed to Theodora, they were running to find something, wanting anything to fill and occupy their terrifying, unfocused energy. She saw how men loved it, loved the exhilaration of forming the gang and running together, the bonding coming in the running. At first when these affrays were just starting, often there wasn't even hatred present. But in the end, of course, hatred always came. They would create it, manufacture it, hurling their insults like weapons up and down streets until the running and shouting turned into real fighting. There was nothing to be done about such surges. They would often stop and peter out as quickly as they had formed. But it was from this set of ingredients that the Kostas boy's death had come. Seen thus it wasn't so extraordinary, wasn't even so appalling. Paul Kostas and his brother had by all accounts contributed their share.

Was it her business, Theodora wondered as she turned from the high street into the narrow road which led first to the church of St Sylvester and then ended in steps down to the river? She recalled Geoffrey's sister, Barbara Brighouse, making a flying visit to the parish soon after she was instituted as deacon. 'Surely this is a terribly inefficient way of catering for social needs,' Miss Brighouse had said, surveying with her competent eye the building works at the church. 'What is really needed is enough money in the social services budget, plus enough jobs to give people some self-respect. Most of these problems,' she waved her hand towards the parish, 'ninety per cent of these problems would disappear overnight.'

'What about the other ten per cent?' Theodora had asked out of curiosity.

'Oh well, I suppose you have to allow a margin for sheer human perversity: wickedness, if you like.'

Theodora was amused. 'Only ten per cent wickedness, ninety per cent misfortune which can be solved by money?'

Barbara Brighouse was a straightforward old-fashioned liberal. She liked efficiency, a good committee, and sensible use of resources. She found little of that in the Anglican Church as far as she could see. She simply could not understand Geoffrey, her favourite brother, joining such a ramshackle body when they had been so close, shared all the important values as children. Three years older than Geoffrey, she had thought she'd taught him better. She turned to Theodora for explanation, for reassurance almost. 'Surely there is no more ineffective way of stopping crime and violence than this. You scarcely touch the surface. Tiny bandages on massive wounds.'

Barbara was so intelligent that Theodora wondered for a moment if she were being ironical. 'But we don't,' she answered. 'We aren't here to imitate the social services. It's not *that* sort of result the Church is looking for. If we start quantifying we're lost. Christianity, any good religion for that matter, offers an alternative reality. Not a patching up of this one. We're here to show people what God is like, where He can be found, what a life lived from and towards Him should, can be. It's another dimension, not a matter of league tables.'

Miss Brighouse had snorted. Really, the woman's a prig, she thought privately. 'Well, it hasn't made much inroads into the world's needs as far as I can see. Frankly I think

Geoffrey is wasting his not inconsiderable talents.' She had paused. 'And you too, my dear.'

'I couldn't be happier,' Theodora had answered.

And it was true, she thought as she rounded the corner and came up against the silhouette of the church outlined against the London sky which was never entirely dark. 'I couldn't be happier.' Then she thought of Mrs Stephanopoulos whom she knew, and Mrs Kostas whom she did not. Someone, somewhere, was thrusting their way through the city, and that someone had killed a boy. Someone, somewhere, was holding captive a girl. And her mind returned again to that odd connection: the Kostases' firm's card on the silver salver at the foot of the statue of the Virgin in the Stephanopouloses' house in Hampstead.

On an impulse, Theodora turned not towards the vicarage and her flat, but towards the ugly brick Victorian house lurking behind the chestnut trees, the Foundation of St Sylvester.

Gilbert Racy turned his beautiful, ascetic profile towards Theodora, whom he disliked. It was not a personal dislike. He disliked most women, but it in no way impaired, he liked to think, his priestly correctness or his effectiveness. He knew their value, and if they could be used to contribute to the quality of the work of the Foundation, he'd use them. St Sylvester's offered a genuine ministry of retreat and healing to those who were sick in mind. Clergy worn down by the intractable requirements of parish life, laymen driven mad by their own and the world's wickedness were catered for. Both Racy's group work and his individual counselling were well organized and, given his many worldly contacts, well resourced. Papers in the journals were not ashamed to quote his findings. He was subterraneanly influential.

Theodora grasped his small single malt with pleasure. She was not sure that she altogether trusted Gilbert. She detected, she thought, a vision which she shared: that people can't be healed but can be put in the way of healing themselves. She thought he knew, too, the difference between healing and cure. He had a perspective which she valued. Nevertheless, he liked power, being able to turn people this way and that, knowing what others did not know. So now she prepared to address herself to him with caution.

'It was in this very room,' Gilbert started out before she could frame her own beginning, 'that Newcome finished *Cities of Men, City of God* in 1879.'

'Really,' murmured Theodora, who had other matters on her mind and, in any case, knew this already. She'd started to investigate the archive. At some point in the future she intended to publish on the life of Thomas Henry Newcome. She thought of Jessica Stephanopoulos. 'I wonder if you could—' she began.

'Of course,' Racy was pressing on in that precise diction, the stress on the first word in a phrase or sentence, which enabled him to be picked out across many a crowded room, 'he knew our problems.'

'Our?'

'The problems of our cities. Listen.'

He reached for the leather volume on his table, took out the floppy leather bookmark which had "The Holy Shrine of Our Lady of Walsingham" etched on it in peeling gilt letters, and began to read. ' "Is any so purblind that he cannot comprehend that the lives lived by the spiritually poor in our great cities draw each one of us, howsoever endowed with worldly riches, towards a common mire? Is it so hidden from our intelligence that if our souls be not properly arrayed, it matters not whether we go in silk and broadcloth or in the veriest tatters?" '

'You see,' Gilbert leaned forward with intellectual passion, 'Newcome can imagine spiritual poverty as afflicting the materially rich quite as much as the poor. Nor does he credit the poor with virtues denied to the rich. He's impartial. In his argument, both rich and poor are impoverished. That's really rather rare in Victorian thought. The temptation to make the rich the baddies and the poor the innocent, or to make the poor vicious, and riches the reward of virtue, is almost always succumbed to. But he's discerning enough to see that it is the *spiritual* poverty of both rich and poor which causes the *material* poverty of the poor.'

Theodora had enjoyed the Latinate cadences of Newcome's prose; of his theology she was less sure. 'So what was his remedy?'

Gilbert chewed his whisky. 'He was ahead of his time there too. Whilst his contemporaries were prattling about moral effort and the will,' Gilbert articulated his contempt for such notions, 'he wanted practices, techniques, artefacts, architecture, a physical setting, to create a tangible Christian culture, to remind us of religious truths and constantly prompt us towards a less destructive, self-destructive life.'

'Hence his church-building activities. Angelic voices. Reminders.'

'Open to rich and poor alike, costing nothing, or only the price of the artefact. Cheaper than television and the advertising which pollute our visual environment and seek to mould our habits and dictate our values,' Racy said, complacently folding his hands over his flat cassocked stomach.

He owned, Theodora realised, very little. He lived as simply as possible. The whisky would undoubtedly have been a present. Whatever reservations she had about Racy, he at least lived the life he preached. Did all St Sylvester's priests do so?

'If we're thinking of visual reminders of the angelic, what do you know about icons?'

'A mistake to think of them as art. They are the products of a community, a believing community, not the lone inspiration of unrooted individual egos. It is noticeable that our own society seems unable to produce adequate or moving works of religious art. Perhaps Pugin was right: you remember. "It is the devotion, majesty and repose of Christian art for which we are contending." Both he and Ruskin knew that religious art can't come out of an unbelieving society.'

On any other night, Theodora would have been happy to follow him down his path. Tonight, however, weighed down by the miserable meeting with Springer and Troutbeck, never able to forget Stella Stephanopoulos's haggard face, she wanted precision, focus and, in the end, enlightenment.

'What do you know of the Greek community?'

'The Kostases?' Racy's tone was neutral. How much did he know, how much had he heard, Theodora wondered.

'Cypriot Greeks are close knit. They have a sense of history second only to the Irish. And of course Greek Orthodoxy is tenacious as an interpretation of the Christian faith. It grips and holds the imagination. Hence its ability to produce its icons.'

'There was an icon on Jessica's dressing table.'

'The Stephanopoulos girl? Is there any news of her?'

Theodora was startled. The press had been silent; Geoffrey was as discreet as any priest who heard confession. 'How on earth do you know?' she asked.

Gilbert looked complacent. 'I have an acquaintance with

one of your St Veep's governors. Ronnie Holdall, he used to be bishop of Bow St Aelfric. Retired a bit before his time when his dean got his throat cut. You may remember.'

Theodora did not care to be reminded. She wrenched the conversation once again back to what she was seeking. 'If you used icons in meditation, as a religious practice, would you need to be taught how to do so?'

'Oh yes, absolutely.' Gilbert had no hesitation, he spoke with the authority of a priest who knew what religious practices demanded. 'Like all religious techniques. If you try to invent the wheel without a teacher you'll come off the rails. That's the point of the church, of course, to keep the techniques pure, the tradition intact. Obviously, I wouldn't deny that such traditions can become corrupted. There's a fourteenth-century manuscript, the Solovki manuscript, which has a commentary on Marian icons which depicts the Virgin's power as a sort of rain goddess. It was her prerogative to send down lightning, frost and earthquakes on the impious unless the prayers of the faithful changed her anger to mercy.'

'Less angelic, more demonic,' Theodora said.

'Weather is a great chastener,' said Gilbert with satisfaction. 'Personally I always like those icons where Mary is shown clasping a ladder and holding a mountain in her hand.' He glanced inquiringly at Theodora.

'Symbols of the links between heaven and earth?' Theodora suggested.

Gilbert nodded. Theodora perceived she had passed some sort of test. Her thoughts went back to Jessica's bedroom. 'Gilbert, would a community, would anyone feel so strongly about an icon, its power and significance that they might kill or kidnap to get hold of one?'

'What had you in mind?' Gilbert suddenly turned his pale eye upon her.

'Oh, nothing. Just that I wondered if there was a connection between Jessica's icon and her kidnapping.'

'Why should there be? She wasn't carrying one around with her, was she?'

'Not so far as I know. It's just that a friend of hers, Clarissa Bennet, made a remark about Jessica being keen on religious art.'

'They're not straight, you know, the Stephanopoulos family.'

'I think I gathered that from what Mrs Stephanopoulos told me. What do you know about them?' Theodora was never surprised at who Racy knew. His network was catholic.

'The grandfather collaborated with the Nazis to get out of prison camp. It wasn't clear what he gave in order to get his favour, but it made him much hated by some of his own countrymen.'

Theodora was glad to have her own inferences from Mrs Stephanopoulos's words confirmed. 'Would that provide a motive for the kidnap of his granddaughter?'

'It might. It just might.'

'I think,' said Theodora as she rose to go, 'I ought to find out more about icons.'

'Try Father Kallistos at the Church of the Resurrection. It's just opposite your school,' was Gilbert's parting shot.

CHAPTER EIGHT

Day School

'Almighty God,' said Dame Alicia curtly, 'give us strength to succeed in our work today; help us to keep our minds on our final achievements. Make us work hard,' she added as an afterthought, lest the Almighty might fail to take her meaning.

Doris King analysed the stylistic infelicities. To the side of the first mistress, Barbara Brighouse, agnostic as she was, rocked to and fro in her staff chair in a paroxysm of embarrassment, groaning to herself under her breath. Down amongst the pupils ranks, the Hapgood profiles elevated into well-bred disbelief like a couple of horses rearing their heads over hedges. They kept a book, a collection of Dame Alicia's failures of tone: it was known in their circle as the *FT* Index.

Dame Alicia's time in the civil service had marked her prose style. She treated God like a dim head of department who needed constant memoranda to keep him on task. She had an ancient Roman attitude to religion. It was God's task to make things better for the creation in fairly concrete ways and not undermine the best efforts of human beings. She worked on the celestial fruit-machine principle of prayer: one put in the token of requests and out popped the prizes of worldly goodies. It said much for the inherited strength of the school that Dame Alicia's prayers had not corrupted it utterly.

Prayers at St Veep's were held daily at nine-fifteen in the hall. It was a highly ritualised occasion, a visual depiction of hierarchy. Those who knew were separated from and seated three feet above those who were still learning. Girls filed in silence into the body of the hall; staff followed at a decent interval and took their places on the platform behind the first mistress. Rank gathered on rank like a tide flooding, until all were gathered. The lower school filled the galleries round three sides. Hymn books and bibles were carried. It had hardly changed as a performance over the one hundred and twenty years of the school's existence. Theodora was surprised to find how it still went on. She was surprised too to find how calming, how comforting the predictable theatre was. It affirmed the community. It was not just a demonstration of authority, not totally risible, and therefore not, in the opinion of those who maintained the ethos of the institution – that set of leathery, determined academic women in senior posts – to be lightly discarded.

When Dame Alicia had first come into the post, Barbara Brighouse had told Theodora, she'd had some crackbrained scheme to 'brighten it up a bit, make it relevant.'

'Can you imagine,' Miss Brighouse had said, 'modern translations of the Bible.'

'The authorised version has a structure of words which has nourished our best minds for four hundred years,' Miss Aldriche had intoned.

'Guitars,' Miss King had murmured.

'Surely not,' Theodora had said, joining in the game.

'Well, perhaps not actually guitars, but certainly taped orchestral.'

'We have, as you may have noticed,' Miss King said kindly to Theodora, 'a perfectly serviceable organ.' She alluded to the nine-hundred-pipe Gloucester and Purvis which would not have disgraced a small cathedral. 'I'll admit some of our organ scholars can be a bit impressionistic at times in their rendering of the hymns, but that doesn't justify . . .'

'A dissonant modernity,' Oenone Troutbeck finished with a flourish.

Doris King shuddered, 'One doesn't want anything too exciting first thing.'

They had all agreed. And in the end they had managed to head Dame Alicia off. They had returned to the tremendously unexciting format of a hymn, a reading, and a prayer chased down by notices about room changes and lacrosse results. It was all very reassuring. Only, no one had yet worked out a way of stopping Dame Alicia from praying.

On this Wednesday morning, two days after the abduction of Jessica Stephanopoulos, the high girlish voices made a good noise. The school's musical tradition was strong. There had been a vigorous rendition of 'Dear Lord and Father of mankind, Forgive our foolish ways' to offset the disappointing results of the first, second, third and fourth lacrosse teams. Sport was one of the few things St Veep's wasn't good at.

Theodora ran her eye along the ranks of her fellow staff. She noticed a little way to her left the small figure of the Reverend Robert Mere. Evidently they hadn't found a place for his talents in the act of worship. The institution's hierarchy was academic, not ecclesiastical. He might be allowed to prepare the confirmation candidates and teach the lower school scripture; more he was not encouraged to offer. However, Theodora reflected, since Jessica was one of his candidates, she would have to have a word with him. Then there was Cromwell, the art master, who was not in prayers, whom she would need to speak to in the light of Clarissa Bennet's remarks about Jessica's interest in religious art. Finally, there was Kallistos Bury in his church across the square who, Gilbert Racy had averred, might know about icons. Given she had a couple of teaching periods to put in, she was going to be busy.

The organ scholar played a marvellous C-major chord to bring everyone to their feet, and started off at breakneck speed with an organ version of the 'Marche Militaire', guaranteed to empty the hall of five hundred girls and staff in under four minutes. The staff avoided the insistent rhythms of the march to show they were not to be dictated to and strolled, ambled or tottered towards their classrooms.

Theodora caught up with the chaplain as he reached the marble entrance hall at the bottom of the stairs. As she approached him, he looked up the flight of steps toward the life-sized cast of the Nike of Samothrace which guarded the top landing. He seemed to feel it barred his way. Theodora had not meant to make him feel as though he was cornered but that was clearly what he did feel. Theodora had no wish to terrify him. But terrified is what he looked as she approached. She wondered whether that was what he normally felt, beset by Valkyries. If that were the case, why did he stay? Was it social snobbery? Was it his wish to be able to say, 'I'm chaplain to St Veep's Girls' School, the best girls' school in England', and did the

licence to say that outweigh the discomfort of being intel-
lectually and socially out of his depth most of the time?
What an uncomfortable way to live.

'Hello,' he said as Theodora came abreast. He placed his
foot on the bottom step. 'Kept meaning to have a word
with you but absolutely up to my eyes this term. Finding
your way about OK? You'll soon get the hang of things.
We're a pretty close community,' he grinned without mirth.
'It's one of our strengths.' He mounted another step.

Theodora was perfectly content to allow herself to be
patronised. She took in his tiny head with its thin hair
brushed moistly down over his ears, and felt a momentary
pity for the man. His eyes were light blue, rather unfocused.
With two steps advantage of her he came up to her
shoulder.

'I wondered if I might have a word with you about
Jessica Stephanopoulos?'

He looked startled; then, Theodora thought,
apprehensive.

'Poor little girl! Where is she now, I wonder? These
political kidnappings. They're just barbarians, these
Greek fellows.'

'You think her disappearance could be political?'

'Not much doubt is there? I mean, her family are foreign.
Greek in fact.'

Theodora nodded. 'Did you know her well?'

'Oh no. Well, she was in my confirmation class.' He
seemed desperate neither to have his cake nor to eat it.
Why was the man so uneasy?

'I understand you taught her on Monday, on the day
she disappeared?'

'Did I? Oh, yes, yes, of course. It's difficult to remember
everyone I teach. Once wrote a report on someone who'd

never been in my class. Left the previous term and no one had taken her name off my list.' He laughed uneasily and hitched himself up another step.

These were not the sorts of mistakes that Theodora made. She repressed her growing dislike of the man.

'What time did you leave school on that day?'

'What?' He looked startled. 'Oh, I see what you mean. Well, yes. To be honest, I had to leave a bit before the bell. I had a very important appointment. Pastoral need. A funeral,' he concluded desperately, taking refuge in the unassailable clerical excuse. 'I told the police.'

'Can you remember anything about the cars waiting outside the school?'

Bob Mere contracted his inconsiderable brow. 'Well, yes. There were the usual ones.'

'Which were?'

'There were the regulars. A couple of Volvos for the Jewish contingent. Then one or two big Fords with drivers or chauffeurs.' He suddenly became confidential. 'The new money have chauffeurs, the old money have drivers like the army. The difference is in the caps. Chauffeurs have caps, drivers don't.' He was delighted to show off his social knowledge. 'Then there were the Mercedes.'

'How many?'

'Um. One, I assume. I mean, I didn't look too closely. It's always there for the Stephanopolous girl. It has a . . .' He stopped and considered. 'I see what you mean. The one I saw didn't have a . . .'

'What?' Theodora asked with exasperation.

'The Greek one has a sort of badge on the windscreen where the tax disc would be. This one didn't have that.'

'Did you notice the driver?'

'Middle aged. Lot of strong-looking black hair brushed

straight back without a parting. No cap,' he grinned in
triumph. 'A driver. Obviously foreign. I suppose Greek.

'But if it wasn't the embassy Mercedes, I mean, didn't
have the badge, would the driver have been Greek?'

'It never occurred to me that he wasn't.'

'But you were expecting him to be.'

Mere sounded even more doubtful than normal. Then
his little face lit up. 'I'm certain he was Greek. He had a
Greek newspaper on the seat beside him.'

'Which one?' Theodora inquired relentlessly.

Kupriakos Alethinos, said Mere, working his New Testa-
ment Greek to its limits.

'Cypriot?'

'I suppose so.'

Theodora let him be. 'Jessica,' she resumed, 'how well
did you know her?'

'Well, not that well. She was new here. I hadn't taught
her from a tot.' He had a rush of confidingness. 'I don't
think she liked me, actually.'

Theodora had to repress asking how unusual that was.
'But you were preparing her for confirmation?'

'They don't have to like me to go through that. The
parents mostly decide it for them.'

Theodora almost liked the man for his honesty. 'Was she
going through a religious phase, would you say?'

'She comes from a Greek background. That's different
from your average Home Counties Anglican. More
extreme.'

'How did it show itself?'

'She used religious things, gew-gaws. I had to set her
right about idolatory.'

Theodora was startled.

'I mean,' Mere said with distaste, 'she kept an icon in

her bedroom.' He made it sound like an exotic pet.

'How do you know?'

'She showed me a copy. She was artistic. She'd done a copy of her icon, the one her grandad had given her. She told us all about it.'

'Did you see it?'

'Oh, yes. She showed it to the class, the confirmation class, that is. It was an annunciation, the Virgin, you know, and all that. Look,' his hunted expression returned, 'I'm terribly sorry, I've got a class waiting. I've got to go.' He glanced up towards the Nike on the landing, took his courage in both hands, and bolted past Theodora up the remaining stairs.

Theodora watched him go. Then she turned briskly towards her own class. She was startled by the slight figure of Miss Whinney, the first mistress's servile secretary, scampering across the marble towards her and obviously bent on conversation.

'Miss Braithwaite, I wonder if you could take a telephone call? It's from the Reverend Geoffrey Brighouse. He's hanging on. You could take it in my room.'

Theodora took the phone from the secretary and heard Geoffrey's familiar clipped tone.

'Theo, this is just to let you know the police took Troutbeck in this morning for questioning and they've charged him with the manslaughter of Paul Kostas.' There was a pause. 'Are you still there?'

Theodora cleared her throat. 'Yes. Yes. What would you like me to do?'

'I've been down to see him. He's in a bad way. He says he's got a cousin, Oenone, at St Veep's. He'd like her to know. Apparently they were close. Can you do that?

'Yes,' Theodora answered, 'yes, I'll see to it.'

Geoffrey looked round McGrath's living room. He

recognised the décor of a lower-deck messroom. It was a bachelor's room with a career behind it. Every available spare inch of wall had photographs, posters, tide-tables or maps on it. There were pictures of naval groups in Malta, Gibraltar, Cyprus and Portsmouth. On the mantelshelf was an array of pottery objects with coats-of-arms on them. From this setting, McGrath emerged every day to face – indeed, Geoffrey thought, to contribute to – a different, a civilian world.

Geoffrey had been in the house twenty minutes. He'd come on immediately after his painful interview with Troutbeck at the police station, in response to a note from McGrath left for him at the school. He'd made his way across the playing field to the back door of the large terraced house, in the basement of which McGrath lodged. It wasn't easy of access. Geoffrey had had to edge his way past an enormous skip parked in the garden, and then descend an iron staircase to the area. A large black and white cat, which reminded Geoffrey of McGrath in build, glared at him before jumping in slow motion up the area wall.

Over the door into the living room, Geoffrey noticed a small wooden crucifix of the sort found in many an Irish household.

'It was my ma's,' said McGrath as he caught Geoffrey's glance. 'She never left Ireland. There were eight of us in a village outside Waterford. When she died that was all she had to leave me.'

McGrath had had something with lunch to sustain him. Conversationally they had beaten about the bush; no progress had been made. Geoffrey shifted uneasily in his bentwood chair. When would they get to the point? He hesitated to rush it but he had a lot to do.

'What's up, McGrath?' For all his efforts, Geoffrey found

it hard to keep his tone from becoming that of an officer to an NCO. He was a priest, he had to remind himself, not a naval officer.

McGrath did not appear to resent this at all. If Geoffrey had but known it, his manner gave him confidence. Geoffrey had been summoned because McGrath reckoned he knew where he was with him. He wouldn't have to explain or justify.

'It's about young Troutbeck. They've got him down the nick, right?'

Geoffrey nodded.

McGrath leaned forward. 'I was twenty-seven years in the service.' The whiskey increased the Irish in his voice.

Geoffrey did not make the mistake of following up the Troutbeck reference. There was no point in doing anything else but letting the man talk.

'Gib, Malta, the States twice. I got around.'

Geoffrey glanced at the map of the world just behind McGrath's head.

'Ship's not unlike schools, wouldn't you say, sir?'

'How d'you mean?'

'They teach you. You've got to give and take. There's rituals. Places you can go, places you can't. Things some can do that others can't. You were an officer. You could do things a CPO couldn't do. On the other hand,' McGrath grinned,' there were things POs could do that it wouldn't be right for an officer to do. Right?'

Get on with it, Geoffrey thought. McGrath gazed back at him, his eyes momentarily focused and keen. His plentiful iron-grey hair was brushed back without a parting, so that it looked like a skull-cap or a helmet.

'Troutbeck and Kostas now, there's a connection.'

Geoffrey didn't move a muscle.

'But they're not a killer and a victim. That's not it. Not in this generation. No, not by a long chalk.' He paused and then went on. 'Young Kostas, both the young Kostases, they had something with them that day. That Monday morning.'

'What?'

McGrath got to his feet and went over to a chest in the corner. He opened the top drawer. There was a powerful smell of camphor. McGrath rummaged for a moment and then brought back a small package which might have been a tobacco pouch. This he laid on the table between them. From it he drew out with great care a photograph, yellow at the edges and cracked from left to right as though often folded. He pushed it under Geoffrey's nose.

'D'you recognise him?' he asked almost belligerently.

Geoffrey studied the faded likenesses. The picture had been taken against a tree and showed two seamen in Royal Navy uniform and a soldier, an officer with insignia not clear enough to recognise. Flanking them, in civilian dress, were two short, strong-looking men with a lot of dark hair who resembled each other. One of the seamen could have been a younger, slimmer version of McGrath. The naval officer next to him Geoffrey did not know, but the young soldier smiling into the camera had a familiar look. Geoffrey raised his eyes from the print and looked inquiringly at McGrath.

McGrath nodded in confirmation. 'My good self, two stone lighter, Commander Dick Pound, my CO, and Captain Jeremy Troutbeck in Cyprus just before the Turks moved in. July '74. Kyrenia harbour.'

'Troutbeck?'

'Building roads with the sappers. Good roads, good blokes. Very different.'

'Related to Ralph?'

'His dad.'

'Where's all this leading, Mike?' Geoffrey never used a Christian name without thought. Theodora would have said he knew what he was doing.

'Got to stick together,' intoned McGrath. 'All Her Majesty's forces. "All arms combined magnificently together". Now is the time for all good men to come to the aid of the party.'

Geoffrey thought: he's further gone in drink than I reckoned. He'd never seen McGrath the worse before.

'Who were the civilians?'

McGrath chewed his false teeth a bit. 'The Kostas twins. Father and uncle of our lot.'

'What?' Geoffrey had no trouble in giving McGrath his reward of astonishment.

'Big shots in Kyrenia, the Kostases. Very influential. You wanted something, they got it for you. Half legit, half mafia. We all knew them. There are things any military or naval establishment needs that can't be got any other way except from the natives. Officers want some things, men want others, like I said. Well, whatever anyone wanted, the Kostases would get.'

Geoffrey knew this perfectly well. 'What did you and Pound and Troutbeck want that the Kostases supplied?' Geoffrey asked with curiosity.

'My own needs were simple,' McGrath said modestly. 'Now Pound and Troutbeck, they had more refined tastes, if you know what I mean.'

Geoffrey wasn't sure he did.

'They were,' McGrath chose his words carefully, 'collectors. Connoisseurs, if you take my meaning. Especially Troutbeck ... They liked old things. Old buildings, bits of china, things you find in antique shops. There's a set of mountains in the north part of the island. On top of each mountain there's a castle, and below each castle you've got a monastery. Neat and symmetrical, you understand. The castles were ruined but the monasteries now, some of them were still in use. Commander Pound and Troutbeck, they spent one leave climbing each of these mountains in turn and visiting the monasteries.'

'I can't see—' Geoffrey unwisely began.

'They came off in a hell of a hurry.' McGrath speeded up his delivery to suit his tale. 'It was an awful mess. Nobody expected it. There wasn't any warning. The Turks rolled down the road on Tuesday 10 July and mopped up as they went. They just herded the Greeks in front of them as though they were herding goats down a road. They picked out the blokes who could fight and put them in camps in the villages – corralled them. The rest, the women and the kids they didn't want, they rolled them back south. Then they stopped.'

McGrath stopped and licked his lips before resuming. 'It's odd, but I hadn't seen any fighting before. At sea you practise for a certain sort of combat, but it's all long-range with guns. You don't expect to have to meet the enemy, eyeball to eyeball. And after all, it was peacetime I joined up. You don't expect violence. It's a shock. No one knows what to do. No one knows the conventions, like. It took time for orders to come through. But we knew our friends. The Kostases. We had to help, naturally. They'd packed everything they had into a couple of trunks and got themselves rowed out to the frigate after dark the second day. Like I said, we hadn't any orders. They had British passports, of course. Commander Pound said to put them in the bow locker room and say nothing.'

'But what . . .?' Geoffrey tried again.

'They brought off what they could. Anything that'd make a price.'

'Like?'

'They knew from Pound and Troutbeck what would sell in the West. And they were easily packed.'

'What were?'

'Pictures. Holy pictures.' McGrath's eye went to his mother's crucifix.

'Icons? How do you know?'

'I organised the transport both ends, didn't I? They had a packing case full of them, and when they got to London they put them through with our luggage and caught them up the other side of customs.'

'And you're saying that's what the Kostases used for capital when they got here?'

'Seems logical.'

'But wouldn't that have made them richer than they appear to be? If they were valuable?'

'Depends how easy they were to dispose of, 'McGrath said judiciously.

'You mean if they were stolen? If the Kostases didn't have a proper provenance for them?'

'Right.'

'So what has this to do with the death of Paul Kostas?'

'Reckon those lads had gone into the trade.'

'Selling icons?'

'They were carrying one round the school in that bag of theirs on Monday.'

'How do you know?'

'I had a look.'

'When?'

'Troutbeck wouldn't let that class take their bags into the lesson. I expect it's difficult to do drama with forty plus

116

holdalls littering the place. So he made them all leave their bags outside. There was an argument. Lad's don't like to be parted from their bags, there being such a lot of thieves about. However, after a bit of argy-bargy they left them. I just happened to be passing and I had a peak at the Kostases' one.'

Geoffrey drew a deep breath. 'Let's get it straight, McGrath. Are you saying that Troutbeck killed one of the Kostases to get his icon?'

McGrath snorted with contempt. 'What, him? He's not the man his dad was. He didn't kill Kostas. He couldn't kill a fly.'

'Who then?'

'Who pushed the Greeks out of north Cyprus?'

'The Turks.'

CHAPTER NINE
Holy Images

Early afternoon light touched the heads of twenty-five of
the pupils of St Veep's, bent, with religious concentration,
over attempts to render the different textures of bread,
wine flagon, candle-stick and linen cloth of the still life
arranged on the table in the middle of the studio. Theodora
took in the space with pleasure. Three walls were bare and
white, the fourth was covered with the colours of pupils'
work. The slight smell of turpentine, the orderly circle of
easels, the white walls and light from a central overhead
window, reminded her of Nonconformist chapels. Had Jessica known and enjoyed its peculiar atmosphere, she
wondered? Of Cromwell there was no sign.

She edged cautiously round the periphery of the room,
unwilling to disturb the pupils' silent concentration, and
made for a door set in the fourth wall and leading, she
surmised, to Cromwell's sanctum. Before she reached it,
the door opened towards her, and through it came Clarissa
Bennet. There was a moment's hesitation on both their
parts. Clarissa eyed Theodora in much the same way as she

had done over the banisters two days ago on Theodora's first arrival at the school. Only this time, Theodora noticed, Clarissa was less composed. Then, with a quick, almost petulant movement, Clarissa turned and made for the door by which Theodora had entered.

Cromwell's room was the opposite of the studio; the vestry, Theodora thought, to the main church. It was smaller, darker, and cluttered with the detritus used for running the main show. There were objects which could have no meaning in themselves – gourds, a colander, a piece of satin cloth – and some such as a mask and a skull which were macabre, which would perhaps take on significance, even beauty, when combined into a still life. Out of nothing, Cromwell's eye, his expertise, would connect and disconnect objects to create a small universe.

Theodora took in Cromwell seated at his table, a wooden board in front of him, a strong smell of cedar oil surrounding him like a halo of incense. Is he priest, magician or craftsman? Theodora wondered. Certainly she was aware of his power.

Cromwell was embarrassed. He got to his feet and sought in vain for a seat for Theodora. None offered. At a loss for a moment, he finally lifted up a pile of blank canvases and disclosed a stool beneath.

'Ah, the she-deacon. Or is it priestess?'

Theodora hated this sort of thing and hadn't yet found a way of dealing with it.

'Is Clarissa Bennet artistic?' she asked by way of revenge. She knew the term 'artistic' would grate on him.

Cromwell thawed a little. It seemed, if she gave as good as she got, he might come round. 'She has an excellent *critical* eye. Her actual execution tends to be derivative.'

'She parodies?'

'In life as well as art, I suspect.'

'Did she know Jessica Stephanopoulos?' Theodora got down to brass tacks. 'I mean, was she a friend?'

'Jessica didn't have friends. She was a solitary, not a conventual.'

'But Jessica was one of your group?'

'She came along to our club meetings, yes. She went on the gallery trips, did the extra bits of work which qualify you for membership of our exclusive women's club.'

Theodora noted how quickly Cromwell was embarrassed, and how he dealt with his feelings by facetiousness. Perhaps, she thought, he's not so formidable as he gives out to be. 'Had your club been on any visits which focused on religious art?'

Cromwell eyed her. It had been a shot in the dark on Theodora's part, but Cromwell might not know that, 'You mean our trip to the Resurrection?'

Theodora looked keen.

'Well, of course, it was her sort of thing. Icons are in her blood. And she was obsessed with them. She'd dozens of copies of them, beautifully done, beautifully observed.' Cromwell was passionate. 'And of course she knew Kallistos Bury, the Greek papa there; so it seemed a good idea.'

'When did you go?'

'First week of term. We trotted down one wet Saturday morning.'

'Who's "we"?'

'Only the art club.' Cromwell looked surprised. 'No point in having an exclusive club if you open it up to the *polloi*.'

'And that would have been?'

'On that occasion I seem to remember two or three middle-school children, Jessica of course, and from the top of the school Clarissa, the Hapgood twins, that charming

121

American girl, Eulalia Topglass, and that irritating child whose uncle is a canon of Exeter which makes her an expert on anything ecclesiastical.'

'Has the Church of the Resurrection got a good collection of icons?'

'The iconostasis isn't outstanding, but being a composite with icons from different places and periods, it's really rather good for teaching purposes.'

'Different places?'

'Well, it's a Greek Orthodox church, of course, but they've got icons from all over the place, donated by different ex-patriot Orthodox communities. There are some Russian and Cypriot ones as well as the Mount Athos factory output.'

'I don't know much about icons.'

Cromwell looked at Theodora as though he thought she might be being disingenuous. Then his enthusiasm got the better of him. 'Look,' he said, 'you can get some idea from this. It's only a copy but still good enough to learn on.'

He got up and went to a press on the other side of the room behind Theodora. Before she could turn to watch him, he had slipped a square object about two foot square, wrapped in oiled linen, on to the table between them. Carefully he unfolded the wrapping to reveal an icon of the Virgin at the moment of the annunciation. The mother of God, in the traditional deep blue mantle against a silver background, was turned outwards to receive the prayers of the faithful. In the top right-hand corner a winged Gabriel, considerably smaller to denote his status, reached down towards her with a gesture which was half designation, half blessing.

Theodora gazed at it carefully for some time. She could see it was a copy, but it was also the product of some skill and, she thought, of love.

'They're wonderful things, aren't they?' Cromwell was warmed by her appreciation. 'Every stage in their making is a religious act. You know how, when a priest vests for a service, he prays particular prayers as he puts on each liturgical garment, so that he's literally clothed in prayer. Well, it's rather like that with an icon. The preparation of the wood on which they're painted, through the mixing of the pigments to the execution of the figures, is the product of a consecrated life. Only monks produce icons. Not nuns.' He grinned maliciously at Theodora.

'And the end product?'

'Highly stylised beauty. No ego, no self-expression, no whimsical innovation. And because egoless, fit for worship, windows to heaven. Creation only from existing elements. Like God.'

'It depends how you interpret the texts,' said Theodora, ever one for accuracy.

'I'm not a theologian, only an artist. Art combines existing elements to make significant wholes.'

'Do your pupils grasp this?'

'Jessica did. Most go for self-expression. No discipline, no self-denial in the modern world.'

Theodora was rather intrigued by this religious view of things from so exuberant and, she had judged, ego-filled a personality as Cromwell.

'Whose is this?' She gestured to the icon on the table.

'It's Jessica's copy of the one she has at home.'

'It's very carefully done.'

'I supervised its every stage,' said Cromwell with satisfaction. 'Jessica knows how to prepare boards, mix pigment and, as you can see, draft. Her spiritual life I am not qualified to comment on, but I'd say there was a glimmer there, wouldn't you?' He glanced sideways at Theodora for an informed opinion.

'Have you seen the original?'

Cromwell looked regretful. 'She wouldn't let me do that. I imagine the family might have objected to her bringing it in, and she, perhaps, didn't quite feel up to introducing me to her family. Her father's a soldier, I gather.' Cromwell seemed to think that this explained Jessica's reluctance.

'Where would a work like this have originated? Could you tell from a copy?'

'It depends how accurate Jessica has been. If she's got it right, it's not the best period, that is, tenth-century Byzantine or twelfth-century Russian. It could be latish, fourteenth century, Greek certainly, by someone who has seen a bit of Italian.'

'Corruption setting in?'

Cromwell grinned. 'As you gather, I like the more austere early stuff rather than the more luscious later. Still – ' he gave a last look at the admirable piece and lovingly replaced the wrapping – 'it's pretty good, all the same.'

'When did Jessica give it to you?'

'Last thing Monday, just before she was snatched. Poor kid. Where on earth is she now, do you suppose?'

Theodora glanced at Cromwell's exaggeratedly beautiful head, its abundant dark hair curling and full, his expression of nobility on a wide brow, his lips chiselled, his chin cleft. He'd be seen as a desirable object of worship by adolescent girls.

'That icon you showed at your lecture; the Virgin and child. Where would the original of that be?'

'It's a slide Jessica gave me. Something she'd picked up on her travels, I suppose. It's a particularly good teaching slide to contrast with the Laslo portrait of your grandmother.'

Theodora considered what she had seen. Jessica had a relationship with at least two icons. She had her own bedroom one, a Virgin & Child, and now this new one of the Annunciation which had moved her enough to make her want to make a careful copy. Where had Jessica found this latter, Theodora wondered. Should she tell Cromwell that she had seen the original of the slide recently and in Jessica's bedroom. She decided against it and instead asked, 'Why did Clarissa Bennet faint at your lecture yesterday?'

Cromwell blushed and shook his head like a horse. 'Probably my magnetic presence,' he said angrily.

Geoffrey strode briskly across the playing fields of SWL Comprehensive towards the two tower blocks of the school. McGrath's words, or rather his hints, preoccupied him. They shed a new light on things. The only question was, did he trust him?

He remembered McGrath's small piggy eyes, veiled in drink, but then suddenly keen and intelligent. He'd an Irishman's delight in a tale, a drama. His talk about past politics provided a background, a landscape of violent events from which it was possible to imagine a concatenation of cause and effect which might lead to the present outrage, the death of a boy. But if so, if McGrath were pointing in the right direction, could McGrath himself be excluded from suspicion? he's been present in Cyprus; he was present at SWL Comprehensive. He'd actually been on the corridor when the boy's death occurred. He really ought to have pressed McGrath for more information, especially about the Kostases. How many of the Cyprus generation were active and still about? Did McGrath keep up with them? Had he indeed renewed an acquaintance with the older Kostases, the original twin brothers whom he'd helped out of Cyprus, one of whom was presumably the father of Peter and Paul?

Geoffrey broke into a trot as his thoughts gathered pace. Would what McGrath had said *help* Troutbeck, or would it increase the possible reasons for the killing? He reflected on what he knew about Troutbeck. Troutbeck was a fish out of water, so to speak. It wasn't clear what he was doing at SWL Comp. If McGrath's tale about Troutbeck's father's connection with the Kostas family was right, had something, some knowledge perhaps, been passed on from father to son which might give cause for Kostas to taunt Troutbeck or for Troutbeck to kill Kostas?

And what of McGrath's cryptic remarks, on which he had refused to elaborate, about Turks? Geoffrey changed gear into a serviceable cross-country canter, his stride lengthening as he settled into a rhythm and rounded the goalposts of the last of the three football pitches. He was sure there would be Turks in Betterhouse, but he was equally sure that he didn't know any. The only Turks Geoffrey knew about were those you prayed for in the collect for Good Friday. Perhaps he'd better check on that. Who would know? Who was nearest to hand? Springer might. Springer had a big network of useless information tapped into that database of his in his awful office. He'd start there.

Before that, however, he really must have a word with the other Kostas twin. Given that his mother had said she didn't know where his father was, and clearly the mother herself wasn't in the know, the Kostas youngster was the only person who probably knew everything Geoffrey needed to know. Needed, that is, if he were to exonerate Troutbeck. It was simply that Geoffrey doubted if he could be made to speak. Still, he must try.

Geoffrey found he'd worked himself up to a splendid

final sprint as he reached his decisions. He pelted across the remaining twenty yards of mud and took the cracked paving towards the glass entrance doors at a punishing pace.

In front of the secretarial guichet with its minatory notice, NO PUPILS BEFORE ELEVEN, Geoffrey stood with his hands on his hips waiting for his breathing to return to normal before embarking on his inquiries. Since the death of Kostas, rules about all visitors reporting to the office had been tightened. In theory the secretary on duty was supposed to survey everyone as they came past the glass. In fact, the secretarial staff were much too busy to do any such thing. When he'd panted his way back to having enough breath to frame his questions, Geoffrey tapped on the glass to attract attention.

A school secretary's tasks are not few. Apart from the day-to-day typing of letters and lists, and the immense amount of work that the DFE had created by its demands for statistical information on everything, from numbers of pupils whose first language is not English to the number of times the boys' urinals were flushed in every twenty-four hours, there are the ongoing demands of pupils who are bleeding from various parts of their anatomies, parents who are angry with the school about pupils who are bleeding, parents who need to see the head, parents whom the head would rather not see, workmen who need to be directed to parts of the building which need their attention, workmen who need to be prevented from attending to parts of the building where it is not convenient for them to be or might be downright dangerous for them to be. The visitors alone could keep a full reception staff busy throughout the day, Education Welfare Officers come early, publishers' reps later, visiting governors at any time so long as it is inconvenient, educational psychologists, peripatetic music staff, and local authority advisers are all regulars. Either you deal with all or you deal with none. Mrs Eveready had chosen the latter course. Her mother had been a good plain cook; Mrs Eveready was a good plain typist. All else, apart from a little first-aid for the juniors, she eschewed.

Geoffrey's arrival posed another problem for Mrs Eveready. The lunch-break stretched from noon to two; the first hour for the juniors, the second for the seniors. Mrs Eveready could never decide which of those hours she was going to take for her own lunch. Whichever she chose made her regretful that she had not chosen the other one. Geoffrey's intrusion at ten-past twelve, therefore, found her poised between choices. Her first instinct was to ignore him, her second to use her technique for sending people away. This involved raising the head very slowly and gazing with incredulity slightly to the side of them.

When she saw that it was an adult and not a pupil, an adult that looked vaguely familiar, a male adult, and finally a male adult with a clerical collar, she revised her tactics. She got up with great energy, used both hands to pull back the frail glass partition, put her head through the opening and said, 'Yes?' very loudly. Geoffrey thought for a moment that she might take him by the ears and swing him about a bit. But he too had his techniques. He brought his face down close to Mrs Eveready's and smiled his entrancing smile.

'I'm so very sorry to interrupt your lunch-time, Mrs Eveready. But I do rather need your expert advice.'

It worked. Mrs Eveready's frustration evaporated. Someone was going to be kind to her. They were not going to blame her. It made a change.

'Reverend Brighouse, isn't it? Come inside. It's difficult to talk through these things.'

'The point is, Mrs Eveready,' Geoffrey assumed intimacy by placing his long forearms on the desk and leaning towards her, 'I need to find young Peter Kostas, Paul's twin. And I also want a word with Mr Springer, if that's at all possible.'

Mrs Eveready became another person. The task required reference to timetables. Timetables she liked: they were steady things which often remained the same for long stretches at a time. It was change which Mrs Eveready hated: change meant choices and she wasn't good at them.

Timetables were produced, alternatives lovingly evaluated. 'Kostas now, tenth year, that equals *either* second lunch or gym club or house group. Provided, of course, he's in school at all,' said Mrs Eveready triumphantly.

Another set of records was produced, this time on the computer screen. 'Yes. We're in luck. He's marked as present. So your best bet is . . .'

Geoffrey thanked her profusely. 'And Mr Springer?' he ventured.

'That's more difficult,' Mrs Eveready admitted. 'He's never an easy man to pin down appointment-wise, if you see what I mean. Tell you what, he usually looks in on senior dinner last thing. You might catch him there.'

Geoffrey started out in his pursuit of Peter Kostas. He made first for his classroom. Geoffrey took the steps in his accustomed manner. The door of the third-floor room, when Geoffrey reached it, was closed and seemed to be a bit stiff. Geoffrey leaned his weight against it and the vandalised lock gave way. His eye met six black youths, all of excellent physique, with playing cards in their hands, sitting round a table made up of four desks pushed together. No one moved or looked at him.

He cleared his throat. 'I was looking for Peter Kostas,' he began. For a moment there was no reply. Then the tallest of the boys turned his head slowly in Geoffrey's direction and said huskily, 'This classroom's black – ' he tapped his wristwatch – 'till two o'clock. Right.'

'Right,' said Geoffrey promptly, and withdrew. Nothing to be got there, it appeared. He hesitated and thought of the gym club, which would presumably be in the gym. He took the stairs down and strode through the double doors of the senior gym. It was unwontedly quiet. There was a sort of rustling flutter at the far end. A number of bodies parted to disclose Cherry Rumbold in the lotus position, fingers in the correct Buddhist fashion, eyes half closed. About a dozen girls, Geoffrey realised, were similarly positioned. Geoffrey was impressed. But the whole group was female; of the young Kostas there was no sign.

That left the dining hall. Even Geoffrey's optimistic spirit quailed at the thought of broaching the senior dining hall. He knew that, even in the best-regulated schools – and the SWL Comp didn't nearly qualify for that status – orderly, disciplined and well-meaning youngsters who'd behaved perfectly acceptably for three hours in the morning would, at the stroke of the dinner bell, be transformed into demons straight from the canvas of Goya.

Guided by the noise, a dull roar punctuated by metallic clashes, he approached the swing doors with trepidation. He was not disappointed. It is not easy to feed fifteen hundred children in three lots, one after the other. The last lot almost inevitably sits in the custard of the first two lots. The air was thick with the smell of rancid fat, the tables awash with tomato sauce, the floor a sea of spurned paper napkins. Humanity, nominally seated at tables of five, leaned, lay, kicked or swung on the furniture and each other. A group of Afro-Caribbeans were practising rap with spoons; a table of matronly eleventh years were adorning each other with make-up; and a solitary, smallish boy was arranging noodles, for which he had clearly no further dietary use, to illustrate the structure of the atom as shown in his physics textbook.

Well, at least, Geoffrey thought, it's full of life; no apathy here. He began to swim his way through the breakers of children's legs, towards what he thought might be the right age-group for Kostas. When he reached his goal, he flung priestly decorum to the winds, reverted to navy tactics, bent down and put his mouth very close to a boy's ear and bellowed, 'Peter Kostas. Where is he?'

'Search me,' said the boy, removing his ear from Geoffrey's range and applying his little finger to it.

The boy opposite him, who had been feeding his girl-friend with bits of pizza, paused momentarily in his amorous attentions and glanced at Geoffrey. 'Left ten minutes ago. Probably bunked off. He don't care for chemistry.'

'Don't care for anything much except clouting people,' said his lady, daintily removing her half-nibbled pizza from her mouth.

Geoffrey nodded his thanks for her courteous help, and began to fight his way back towards the doors. As he reached them, Springer slid through, his false athleticism useless to him in real life. A posse of girls, leaving the hall three abreast and intent on harmonising the words of a song, caught him full in the chest.

'Oops, sorry guv,' said the outrider as her elbow made contact.

'That's quite OK, Shirl,' said Springer heartily. He knew the name of every one of his fifteen hundred pupils, he would boast to his governors and LEA masters.

'I'm Sharon,' the girl called back in disdain over her shoulder as she swept down the corridor.

'She's a great joker,' said Springer, smiling affably towards Geoffrey.

'Headteacher,' Geoffrey accosted him. He could not bring himself to call him Lance and he didn't like him enough to call him Springer. 'Could you possibly give me a minute or two? It's about young Kostas.'

CHAPTER TEN

Modern History

Oenone Troutbeck bent the rear-view mirror of her Volks-
wagen Golf towards her and adjusted her earrings.
Theodora, in the passenger seat beside her, was aware of
her scent and the absolute propriety of her soft, grey-
brown tweed suiting. Oenone was distressed, otherwise she
would never have adjusted her *toilette* in public. They had
driven down to Betterhouse from St Veep's as soon as
possible after the end of afternoon school.

'I can't think why the police won't bail him,' she said.

With anyone else, Theodora would have supposed her
near to tears. They had spent a terrible two hours at the
police station waiting to see Ralph. It had required an hour
and a half in a police waiting-room, and twenty minutes
with a distraught Ralph who kept on saying, 'The police
don't understand me. They can't seem to grasp my syntax.
Every time I read what they call my statement, they make
me say a whole lot of things I haven't said and haven't
done and wouldn't have expressed in that way if I had.'

'I think they won't bail him until they've got a statement

from him.' Theodora knew enough of police procedure
to offer.

'It's a pity his father isn't about,' said Oenone, 'Uncle
Jeremy was fairly forceful in situations like this.'

'Where is your uncle?' Theodora inquired.

'Shot by a sniper in Kenya in '81,' said Oenone briskly.

'I'm sorry.'

'Well, it's what military families have to live with: constant danger and sudden death. I must say I can sympathise
with poor Stella Stephanopoulos.'

'Did you know her?'

'I met her when Jessica was taking the entrance examination. We got on rather.'

'Yes,' said Theodora, who saw that they might well have.
'Look, would you care to have a bite with Geoffrey and
me before your trek home?'

'I could use a large G and T.'

'Turn left at the lights.'

Theodora wondered, as they pulled up in the high street
outside the Paradise Garden restaurant, whether this was
quite the sort of place Oenone was going to feel at home
in. The proprietor, known as Harry, had an oriental taste in
décor. The place was advertised by a red neon sign showing
a palm tree and water cascading from a fountain. Inside,
Harry liked anything ornate, shiny, or plush. There was a
great deal of this type of thing crammed into the long
narrow corridor which was his dining room. They ducked
under low-hanging, multi-coloured Venetian lights, circled
brass cauldrons filled with trailing plants on tripods with
curly legs, and gained the purple silk banquette next to the
miniature bar at the far end.

They were, however, known. Theodora and Geoffrey ate
there once a week as a relief from bacon sandwiches or

parish hospitality. It was early in the evening: there were no other diners. Harry was, therefore, effusive, deferential and welcoming. Oenone liked to be with people who were greeted by restaurant proprietors, which made Theodora wonder whether Oenone was quite as sophisticated as she appeared.

Geoffrey, already installed, rose to greet them. 'Miss Troutbeck, how very kind of you to join us. You must be absolutely exhausted. What will you drink?'

Oenone expanded like a Japanese flower in water in the presence of a personable man. Theodora could see her relax and glow. Gin and tonics and sherry were produced without pause by a waiter so good he was invisible. Oenone was impressed. The evening boded well. Explorations were made by Oenone in her usual style. Geoffrey, brother, of course, of good old Barbara. A clerical family perhaps, with a kind glance at Theodora. No? A naval one. Even better, in Oenone's eyes. Had Geoffrey by any chance run across Admiral Pillinger? Geoffrey had, so all was well.

Geoffrey waved away the invisible waiter proffering the enormous menu, and smiled his lovely smile at Miss Troutbeck. 'Will you allow me to order for us?' he inquired.

Theodora was conscious of a pang of what could only be called jealousy. Damnit, who helps him run his parish, Oenone or me? She convicted herself instantly of being absolutely childish. It's odd, she thought, how atavistic, how totally unallowed for one's instincts were. She coveted Geoffrey not at all, admired his professionalism, respected and shared many of his attitudes, and wanted no more of his attention than a smoothly running working relationship required. She had plans for her immediate future which certainly did not require Geoffrey's full-time notice. Yet here she was troubled by a stab of resentment. Surely it was from such an unguarded cave that terror and violence sprang. From just such had come Kostas's death and Jessica's kidnap.

Geoffrey was right, however, she reflected, to keep the ordering of food in his own hands. It would be folly to let an amateur wade through the fantasy of Harry's menu. He served only one sort of meat: it was kid. Sometimes it was called chicken, sometimes lamb, sometimes rabbit. But actually it was always kid and, if you picked right, always delicious. Where Harry got kid from in south London – where indeed he himself hailed from – wasn't too clear to Theodora. Armenian, was he, or Macedonian? His was another family concern with an unlimited supply of dark-haired sons, cousins and nephews, seemingly identical in shape and feature, glimpsed in the kitchen, remarked behind the bar, hardly noticed when serving and present to help with coats at the final exit. The only difference between the younger members of the family and the older ones like the barman, she observed, was that the older ones tended to have the dark shadow of a too-potent beard if one came late in the evening.

Salads of yoghurt and cucumber came; warm pitta bread came; then the kid (rabbit, lamb) in its sauce of tomatoes and garlic, with beans and peppers just discernible. A purple, sweetish wine followed in a bottle labelled 'Venus'.

Conversation languished. Bodily needs were more than satisfied. There was a pause. Oenone asked charmingly if she might smoke. Geoffrey, who did not, practically fell over himself to light her up from the tiny candle on the table. Then he began.

'I wonder if it might help if we were to pool our knowledge?'

Theodora's resentment evaporated. They were back to business; she recognised Geoffrey's methods.

'If you think I might know anything which could help poor Ralph, of course.' Oenone sounded perfectly genuine.

'How is Ralph bearing up?'

Oenone glanced at Theodora. 'Well, actually, not too well. He's not the strongest of characters. I mean, one doesn't want to use terms like "neurotic" of one's own family but being accused of murder or manslaughter, or whatever they've decided to settle on, is rather annihilating. Thank God his mother's dead.'

'The great thing is motive,' Geoffrey said cautiously, 'and the next is opportunity. Ralph did have opportunity, but would he have motive?' He raised an eyebrow in Oenone's direction. 'And then there's the Aristotelian category of predisposition, hexis. Would Ralph have the sort of predispositions which could result in violence?'

Oenone played with the stem of her glass before replying. 'Ralph isn't well, he's not entirely reasonable. I think Uncle Jeremy bullied him a bit. I remember rows when I stayed with them in the holidays. That sort of thing. It made Ralph into – well, it made him evasive. I suppose a bit of a liar, really, just to avoid trouble. He was a serving soldier, Uncle Jeremy.'

Oenone sounded as though she was searching for a defence of her uncle.

'I know Aunt Ginny felt he was far too hard on Ralph. I thought he'd found his feet at Cambridge, made his friends and so on. We overlapped, of course. But his career's never really taken off. He tends to side with underdogs, naturally, but his tastes, his background, make him impatient with and unsympathetic to the really deprived. He desperately wants to be one of them, but then he doesn't really like their manners, their attitudes. Twain meeting, and all that.'

Theodora suddenly realised that Oenone was not without

self-knowledge, and that her snobbery might be a sort of heroism, an unwillingness to pretend to attitudes she knew she would never share. As for her words about Troutbeck, they sounded convincing to Theodora from what she'd seen of him. But that was still some way from killing a boy.

'Do you know Ralph well enough to be able to say whether he could kill a boy?' Geoffrey's tone was so gentle, the horrific implications of this question might well have escaped Oenone. Certainly she was lulled into honesty.

'I suppose if I'm frank, if young Kostas was bullying Ralph, Ralph might have hit him, pushed him or something. I don't think Ralph's murderous, but he can run on a short fuse. Of course, in an independent school, it would hardly matter, but I expect it does down here.'

Theodora forbore to remark that, even in an independent school, you couldn't go around killing pupils who annoyed you.

'Did Ralph know the Kostas family?' Geoffrey asked. 'I mean, outside school?'

'Why?'

'I had a talk with McGrath, the school caretaker, this morning, at his invitation. He told me that your uncle had had dealings with the Kostases in Cyprus about the time of the Turkish invasion.' Geoffrey filled in the details. Theodora listened carefully, watching Oenone's beautiful regular profile.

When he'd finished there was a pause. Then Oenone said, 'Your man, McGrath, is it? Is he reliable?'

'I don't honestly know. He must be a suspect too in terms of opportunity. He was on the same landing as the class at about the right time, at the other end of it, on his own account, mending chairs in his workroom.'

'McGrath's right about Dick Pound and Uncle Jeremy

being friends,' Oenone conceded. 'There are lots of photographs. He's also right about Uncle Jeremy being a collector. I'm not sure his taste was aesthetic so much as antiquarian. He liked really odd or grisly objects, serpents-with-skulls-in-their-jaws-type stuff.'

I'm not surprised Ralph was frightened of his father, Theodora thought.

'I don't know what he brought out of Cyprus. I don't remember anything like icons in the house. I do know that when he died some of his stuff went to Dick Pound.'

'Would it be worth inquiring what that was?' Geoffrey asked.

'I thought Pound was dead,' Theodora said, recalling her Uncle Hugh. 'I told you so,' she looked at Geoffrey.

'Yes,' said Oenone. 'Quite true. He crashed in the jungle about two years after Uncle Jeremy was shot.'

'Who would have got his stuff?' Geoffrey went on like a hound, Theodora thought, watching him keep to his line of inquiry.

'His wife, surely,' Oenone answered, 'Dame Alicia.'

Geoffrey turned towards Theodora. 'Ah, how very convenient. Theo, I wonder if you could make inquiries?'

'No,' said Theodora. 'No really, Geoffrey, I couldn't. I've only spoken to Dame Alicia once – or rather been spoken to by her. She told me what a great opportunity it was for me to be allowed to teach at St Veep's, and what a lot of famous people sent their talented daughters to the place. And that was it. I really couldn't, on the strength of our acquaintance, ask her what was in her dead husband's effects.'

Geoffrey's expression suggested her scruples were unreasonable but would have to be indulged. He turned back to Oenone. 'Oenone?'

'I suppose the question might look more natural coming

from me,' Oenone admitted. 'What would be the significance? I mean, what is the connection between Uncle Jeremy's effects, say an icon which originated from Cyprus, even from the Kostas family, and the death of their boy?'

Theodora couldn't help but admire the way Oenone had threaded her way through a narrative which, to be honest, Geoffrey had left her to infer rather than made explicit.

'Well, I can't quite see my way yet,' Geoffrey admitted. 'But I had a word with Springer after I'd done with McGrath. I asked him if he thought what McGrath said about the Kostas twins carrying an icon round with them might be true. He hummed and hawed a bit but finally he said he'd thought for some time that the brothers were used by their dad as a sort of safe deposit for goods which presumably for one reason or another Kostas père didn't want to keep at home for a space.'

'How'd he know?' Theodora was curious.

'Springer circles round the school in the off-hours. It's his way of keeping in touch. He can't teach, so his only way of knowing even vaguely what's going on is a bit of snooping. He'd come on the Kostases last term defending themselves against a bit of peer-group pressure in the locker room. Only he'd been scared because one of the Kostases had had a knife and of course his dad had just done six months for taking a knife to one of the Vouniki clan. Springer was apprehensive that he might have something serious on his hands so he'd reported it to the governors. They'd gone to three days exclusion, but hadn't called the police or anything.'

Theodora thought back to the meeting with Springer the other evening. 'What had the Kostas boys been defending with the knife?' she asked. 'Did Springer know?'

'He couldn't make them hand over whatever it was there

and then, but he'd questioned them the next day in the presence of his deputy and he thought it might have been a collection of medals or something, because they'd spoken of defending the honour of their family. I got the impression that Springer was unfamiliar with their concept of honour, knowing their background, but took it to mean military reputation.'

'So what you're saying is that the Kostas twins had a habit of – and a reputation for – carrying valuables round the school in their bags, and that this might have given a cause for the killing, either accidental or intended, of one of them,' Oenone summarised.

'Would that someone be inside the school or outside?' Theodora asked, thinking of McGrath.

'The school's very easy to get into,' Geoffrey said. 'It has two blocks: the junior block, which is more or less obscured with builders' scaffolding at the moment; and the senior one. The death took place in the senior one. The side entrances are locked after the main influx at nine a.m. Then latecomers and visitors are supposed to report to the office just inside the main doors of the senior block. They are, of course, understaffed. My impression is that people come and go pretty much as they please. And of course when there are workmen about it's particularly difficult to keep tabs on them.'

'You mean, pretty well anyone could have walked in and got at the Kostas boy.' Oenone looked more cheerful than hitherto. 'If only we could persuade the police to look further afield than Ralph. If only they'd bail him. He might know something, something about his father perhaps. I do hate to think of him in that smelly place.' Oenone's nose wrinkled at the memory of the police waiting-room.

'How about another mouthful?' Geoffrey said with

immense tact. 'A little fruit, a sorbet to cleanse the palate? Some coffee?'

The invisible waiter appeared on the instant at his elbow. Sorbets came; goat cheese came; hot coffee came and a cold, sweet white wine labelled 'Aphrodite'.

Oenone turned suddenly to Theodora. 'Have you any news on the Jessica front? I gather Anne Aldriche asked you to look in on Stella.'

Theodora admired Oenone's intelligence. 'No, nothing. Though it's odd, isn't it, that she too was interested in icons. Indeed, she possessed a rather beautiful one given to her by her grandfather.'

Oenone nodded. 'She passed round a copy of it at her confirmation class. Something to do with the art club.'

'No,' Theodora said with unusual emphasis. 'No. The copy which she gave to Cromwell just before she was kidnapped was not a copy of the icon in her room. The one in her room was of a Virgin and child. The one she gave Cromwell was of an annunciation. Cromwell thought it was a copy of her own icon, and presumably that was what Jessica had told him, or perhaps let him infer. But I remember that the one which Stella Stephanopoulos showed me in her room was quite different. The other one, the Virgin and child . . .' Theodora stopped. She really didn't want to share with Oenone the knowledge that Cromwell had shown a slide of the Virgin and child kept in Jessica's bedroom.

'So where did she get the one she copied to give to Cromwell?' Geoffrey inquired.

'I wish I knew. I wondered at first if she had copied something from the Church of the Resurrection which she'd visited with the art club earlier in the term. But when I'd finished with Cromwell this morning I went across and

looked in the church. I couldn't find anything remotely like
it, and indeed if there had been anything like it, Cromwell
would surely have noticed it.'

'Would there be icons there which weren't on show?'
Geoffrey inquired.

'I tried to get hold of the priest, Kallistos Bury. He's an
acquaintance of Gilbert's. Gilbert Racy,' Theodora explained to Oenone, 'runs the retreat house of St Sylvester's
next door to our church.'

Oenone's interest had fallen back to the merely polite.
Her cousin's plight interested her, Jessica's did not, or at
least not in the same way.

'Did you get anything from him?' Geoffrey asked. Since
he had got from Oenone her promise to delve into the
Pound/Troutbeck connection, he was more relaxed about
Theodora's problems. Theodora, however, felt that
Geoffrey had done his bit for Troutbeck, and now she
wanted him to give a similar consideration to the Stephanopoulos affair.

'I didn't actually get to meet Bury,' she went on deter-
minedly. 'His housekeeper told me he was away on retreat
for Lent.'

Theodora recalled the unsatisfactory conversation with
the shrivelled Greek woman in the house next to the Resurrection. She had not even been allowed over the threshold. 'All I learned about Jessica was that she was part of
a group which met once a week to learn how to use icons
in prayer.'

Geoffrey looked briefly interested.

'I thought she was being confirmed as a Anglican,'
Oenone said with distaste. 'How duplicitous these Greeks
are.'

Theodora leaned across the table. She was determined

to compel his interest. 'Geoffrey, there's one other odd thing about the Stephanopoulos case: the driver of the kidnap car was a Greek Cypriot. He was reading *Kupriakos Alethinos*.'

'Really?' Geoffrey's tone was neutral. 'How do you know?'

'The school chaplain passed close enough to the kidnap car to get a clear view. And there's one other thing. The Stephanopoulos family use the Kostases' transport firm.'

'Use?'

'Well, they had a business card on their salver in the hall with the Kostases' firm's name on it.'

'More than one Kostas transport firm perhaps?'

'Not with a south London telephone number on it.'

'What are you suggesting?'

'I just wondered if there was someone collecting icons.'

There was silence as they all digested this hypothesis. 'By the way,' Theodora asked finally, 'did you manage to get hold of the other Kostas twin?'

Geoffrey looked conscious for a moment. 'No, I agree that it might make things easier if I could get him to talk. I'd just about got myself geared up to go and see the Kostas family after I'd had my go with Springer and McGrath. But when I mentioned it to Springer, he said Mr Kostas had rung in earlier in the morning to say that he wanted Peter to leave school at lunch-time and that he'd be away from school for a bit.'

'Did he give any reason?'

'He said he had business and he was taking the boy with him.'

'Where?'

Geoffrey looked even more uncomfortable. 'Springer said he rather thought Cyprus.'

CHAPTER ELEVEN

Ancient History

When Theodora checked the ansaphone on their return to the vicarage, the voice on it was very quiet. It said. 'Message for Miss Braithwaite, timed at twenty-one-twenty, Wednesday, from Stella Stephanopoulos. It was so good of you to talk on Monday. We've had no further news, but I wondered if we could possibly meet tomorrow, Thursday. Perhaps you could call and tell me times and places convenient for you?'

Theodora played the message through twice. The second time Geoffrey halted in his passage through the hall and listened. 'I suppose her phone's being tapped,' he said.

The same thought had occurred to Theodora. For a moment she felt a frisson of fear. '*Would* something have happened to Jessica, do you suppose?'

'Pray,' said Geoffrey firmly. 'There's nothing more you can do until you see Mrs Stephanopoulos. Ring now and say where you'll meet her.'

At least Geoffrey's taking the Stephanopoulos problems

seriously, Theodora thought, as she lifted the phone to make contact with Mrs Stephanopoulos's answering machine.

On Thursday morning Stella was late. Theodora leaned against the double doors of the front entrance to St Veep's. From there she could command a view of the whole square. She eyed the broad pavement immediately outside the school. It struck her there would be room for no more than four cars here at any one time; the rest would have to line up round the square. To her left was the gate for the seniors, to her right the one for the juniors. The shrubs in the gardens of the brown brick villas of the square were beginning to be brushed with green. Forsythia, garish and early, showed. At the far end of the square she could just glimpse the white portico of the Church of the Resurrection.

Where, she wondered, was Jessica; far away or near at hand? Had anyone in the houses seen anything peculiar on Monday afternoon? For a moment she almost envied the police and their resources. Surely some information would be forthcoming soon. People couldn't just disappear into limbo.

When Stella did appear she was on foot, accompanied, as far as Theodora could tell, only by the bull terrier. He greeted Theodora as an acquaintance of long standing.

'Would it be a good idea to talk in the church? It should be fairly secluded,' Stella indicated the opposite side of the square.

They walked round, the three of them, in silence. The only sound was of their different footsteps: Theodora's, firm and measured, acted as base to the soprano of Stella's tapping and hurried treble, and the rasping of the terrier's nails on the pavement.

Secure as it seemed in the shadow of the portico, they hesitated for a moment. Stella broke the silence between them with, 'Do you know this church?'

'Yes,' said Theodora. 'I came here yesterday.'

'May I ask why?'

'I came to try to talk to the priest, Kallistos Bury. Your daughter, Jessica, had a passion for icons. She was attending a group of his which was studying how to use icons as a device for prayer and meditation. Did you know that?'

Stella hesitated. 'I sort of guessed there was something like that. Of course Kallistos Bury was known to us. He's on the embassy list. He's not Greek. He's a convert. Rather an intellectual young man. He seems to have read himself into Orthodoxy while at Oxford and then gone for the Orthodox priesthood.'

Theodora silently digested the information. 'Jessica also came here with the art club one Saturday earlier in the term to study the iconostasis,' she said. 'Perhaps you knew?'

Stella nodded.

'I wondered if her passion had any connection with her disappearance?'

Stella didn't answer. Instead she secured the dog's lead to an iron hoop at the base of one of the pillars, pushed the small door set in the large one and plunged inside. Theodora followed her. With neo-classical churches, Theodora reflected, there was always an even chance of their being dark. It depended what the nineteenth century had done to the windows: if they had replaced the clear glass with stained, it would be dark. But Theodora knew this was not the case here: she was prepared for the stage-set which opened out before them. The nineteenth century had left the windows alone. The door swung to behind them, and they beheld the large drawing room, flooded with noonday light. The coffered ceiling gleamed white and gold; the white marble floor gave back the light; the pews which had originally ruled out the space of the interior had been swept aside by the requirements of the Greek Orthodox liturgy. A single huge brass chandelier depended from the nave ceiling just in front of the iconostasis. The silence was absolute.

Stella and Theodora stood for a moment, breathing in the incense-laden air, bonded together by light and silence.

'If only it could always be like this,' said Stella, almost whispering.

They settled on a couple of chairs pushed against the wall at the back of the church. Reluctantly Theodora turned to her task.

'Was there any special reason you asked me to meet you today?'

Stella nodded. 'This,' she said, and produced from her bag a small brown envelope. There was no address on it, but typed in Greek characters were the words 'Stella Stephanopoulos'.

Theodora opened it. Inside was a piece of cheap writing paper, to which had been pasted words extracted from a Greek newspaper or magazine. Theodora gazed at the familiar Greek characters for a moment. Then she turned to Stella in surprise. 'But I don't understand. What do they mean?' Theodora translated literally lest she should have mistaken something. ' "You will give us the two holy icons. We will give you again your daughter. You must give us the two so that we shall give you all your daughter without harm. You must do this within three days. You have our gratitude so you do not inform those in power. We will send you a certain message." ' Theodora paused. 'What do they mean? Who sent it? When did it come?'

'It came yesterday, Wednesday,' Stella answered quietly, 'about seven in the morning. Before the morning post which, by the way, the police are handling. It must have come by hand therefore. The maid said she found it on the mat when she came down first thing.'

'And do you know what it means, what it refers to?'

Stella spread her hands in a minute gesture of helplessness.

'What does your husband say?'

Stella looked shocked. 'Of course, I haven't told him.'

'Why on earth not?'

'He would be very angry. I cannot cope with George's anger.'

Oh dear, oh dear, Theodora thought. How very difficult this is all going to be. Why on earth didn't Mrs Stephanopoulos trust her husband and confide in him like any normal married woman? But then, Theodora knew, there were no normal marriages, and trust and confidence between people were the exception not the rule.

She tried again. 'And the police?'

But she knew the answer before it came. Instead Stella burst out. 'They can have the icon, of course. What's an icon? But they say they want two. I don't understand.'

'By icon,' Theodora said, 'they presumably mean the one in Jessica's room, the one her grandfather gave her.'

'I suppose so,' Stella was near to tears. 'But God knows what they mean by two. I rang you because you're so knowledgeable. I thought you might know what they had in mind. I mean religious art, I know so little about these things. I was sure you'd know what to do.'

Theodora was used to people trusting her and overestimating her knowledge, but not to quite this extent. Stella had given her so little information.

'It's all so unfair,' Stella said turning her tearful face towards Theodora. Theodora fixed her gaze on the icon-ostasis, which was full of icons, but did not presumably contain the one the kidnappers wanted from the Stephano-pouloses. There was, she thought, something odd – indeed something irritating – about Stella's whole demeanour which puzzled her.

'The icon which Jessica has: you say it's not valuable. How do you know? Have you had it valued?'

Stella was prompt, 'Oh yes, when we first came over we had everything done by Lancaster and Phelps for insurance purposes. It's worth about two thousand pounds on the present market.'

'Surely not worth going to the trouble of a kidnap for?'

'No, I wouldn't have thought so,' Stella agreed.

Theodora had another thought. 'Who knows that Jessica has an icon in her room?'

Mrs Stephanopoulos did her well-known hand-spreading act. 'Well, I suppose the family and the servants.'

'I really meant of her own friends or outsiders.'

Stella was again helpless. 'She doesn't have too many friends. I suppose Clarissa Bennet might, I think she's the only one who's come to the house out of her school acquaintances.'

'Ah,' said Theodora, thinking of the recumbent form of Clarissa in the medical room. 'But, I still don't see why anyone should want the icon if it isn't valuable.'

'Oh, politics,' said Stella vaguely.

'How do you mean "politics"?' Theodora was almost angry. What was the woman holding back?

'I suppose in some communities things, objects . . . Icons have a symbolic value which is greater than their market or their aesthetic value.'

Theodora again had the feeling she was being played with. 'Do you know any such community which might be willing to pay over the odds for an icon which had a special significance for them?'

Stella shook her head. 'That wasn't what we had in mind.'

Theodora was exasperated. 'I don't understand you. Who is "we" and what did you have in mind?'

Stella turned her beautiful head towards Theodora. 'We can't always choose,' she said. 'But we have to carry on as though there really is a society which is sane and just and which can judge and deal with our terrors. I thought religious people knew that and that if one knew it one could make sacrifices. Do a deal, as it were.'

Theodora wasn't sure where all this was heading. Perhaps it represented the makeshift raft of someone who had to float around in a society to which she did not by birth and temperament belong, and who had had to make her own provision for coping with things which she did not care for. Greek society, Theodora was prepared to believe, was very different from middle-class English. About one thing, however, Theodora was perfectly clear.

'Making sacrifices,' she said firmly, 'isn't, really isn't, the same as doing a deal. And if you've a mind to do a deal with icons to retrieve Jessica. I really do think you should tell both your husband and the police before you go in any deeper.'

'I can't,' Stella wailed. 'I can't. I may never see Jessica again. You don't understand how these people go on and on hating from generation to generation. It's not like England where we don't know any history and we forget our defeats as quickly as our victories. In Greece, in George's family, when he was in Cyprus . . .'

Mrs Stephanopoulos stopped. Now we're getting somewhere, Theodora thought. 'I think you said you were in Cyprus not long before Jessica was born, just before the Turkish invasion,' she prompted.

Stella felt able to nod.

'What exactly was your husband's job there?'

'His job is to carry out government policy,' Stella answered as though by rote.

'Of course,' Theodora was soothing. 'What exactly was Greek government policy at that time?'

'Government policy was to welcome enosis, the incorporation of Cyprus into Greece proper.'

'And George's part in that was to do what?' Theodora had no intention of letting Stella off the hook.

'He was supposed to build up pro-Greek feeling. Pride in things Greek: nationhood and all that.'

'So what you're saying is that your husband made enemies in Cyprus who might want to avenge themselves on his daughter?'

'Oh, but we made many friends there too,' Stella was adamant.

'Whom especially did you make an enemy of?'

'Well, I suppose none of the Turks particularly liked what we were doing. I can't remember any particular names or persons. It wasn't quite my affair.'

'But your husband . . .' Theodora paused.

'I'm absolutely certain that George is doing all he can, "pulling out all the stops", is how he puts it. The ambassador rang today . . .'

Hell's teeth, Theodora thought. Not that again. What's wrong with the woman?

Stella was near hysteria. To give her something else to think about, Theodora went on firmly, 'There are one or two things I wanted to ask you about the details of the actual kidnap.'

Stella appeared to try and get a grip on herself.

'One of the witnesses says he saw only one car outside the school about three-thirty on Monday, and it wasn't your embassy car. What time would your driver have got to the school, do you know?'

Stella hesitated. 'Michel says he was there in plenty of time to pick Jessica up: about ten to four, I think. Anyway, she was late.'

'Did Michel stay there all the time he was supposed to be waiting, or did he go away and come back or leave the car at any time?'

'No, he said he was there all the time.'

'And where was he exactly in relation to the kidnap car?'

'He says his was the last of the spaces immediately outside the school, and the kidnap car was behind him at right angles, the first one on the corner. You see there is only space for—'

'Yes,' said Theodora, 'yes, so I see. Stella, how does Michel come to have a British passport when he speaks so little English?'

'He's Greek Cypriot,' said Stella. 'He came out in '74 with his family. His brother came to England but Michel went on to cousins in Greece.'

'What's Michel's surname?'

'Kostas,' said Stella.

'And do you happen to know what his brother does for a living?'

'Oh, yes. He's got a small transport business in south London somewhere. Michel sometimes uses their vehicles.'

Theodora didn't know whether to grin or cry. How much ought she to tell Stella? Indeed, how did the information Stella had given her fit into the other bits of information which she had about Paul Kostas's death? She very much wanted to get away from Stella and think and then perhaps discuss matters with someone utterly sane, like Geoffrey.

Theodora was reduced to looking at her watch. Stella turned towards her, quieter now, but still unresolved. 'What do you think I should do? I mean, about the kidnap note and the second icon?'

Theodora had an inspiration. 'Some time before she was snatched, Jessica made a copy of an icon. Not the one in her bedroom – another one, an annunciation. Nobody seems to know where the original of that one is. Anyway, she gave this copy to her art master, Cromwell, on Monday afternoon, just before she was kidnapped. Why not offer it to her kidnappers if they make contact again? I'm sure Cromwell could be induced to give it up.'

Stella's face, at first dubious, eventually lit up. 'What a marvellous idea! You are brilliant.'

Together Stella and Theodora left the church and walked out into the sunlight. The bull terrier had slipped his lead and was happily rootling amongst the dustbins at the rear.

Miss Aldriche snapped the light on. Six of the school's former first mistresses, illuminated by striplights over their frames, sprang into view on the wall of the darkening library. Most were in full academicals and larger than life-size.

'I'm afraid your grandmother isn't in the front rank,' she said to Theodora, and snapped another switch. This time a collection on the opposite wall came into view. 'We keep the benefactors separate.'

Theodora walked to the centre of the room and gazed first at the academic portraits, then at the benefactors. On the whole the benefactors were the more interesting. Some were no more than sepia photographs; some charcoal sketches; some, like her grandmother, full-length paintings.

'Dame Alicia has yet to be rendered,' said Miss Aldriche neutrally.

Theodora switched her gaze back to the first mistresses. 'Do we need to make statements like this?' she ventured.

'You feel we reinvent traditions which are not ours?' Miss Aldriche hazarded.

'Something like that.'

'Never underestimate the power of the symbolic. The gentlemen never have. We still have a long way to go. The continuing subordination of women in society is bad for women, bad for men, and bad for society.'

Theodora, who was a subordinate in a mostly male and certainly non-rational hierarchy and who did not actually mind too much since it gave her scope for her sort of sacrifice, didn't feel in a strong position to comment on this.

She took the measure, however, of Miss Aldriche's strength. This, she realised, was the difference between St Veep's and SWL Comprehensive. Here were directive intelligences working out a coherent set of values which, whether you sympathised with them or not, were intentionally shaping the institution for a known future. In the case of SWL it was no one's duty to sift the values and approve the vision, so they fell victim to mere fashion.

Theodora had no wish to be ungracious. It was, after all, a delight to be in an environment where scholarship was valued as a proper activity for women. 'I expect you're right,' she said.

Miss Aldriche turned in stately fashion towards the door. 'Your grandmother's material is in the case beside the *OED*. It's some time since I looked at it, but I seem to remember some excellent observation in her diaries of Egypt and Iran in the late 1920s. She wasn't a scholar, but a lively and humane intelligence – which we exist to nurture.'

As the door swung shut behind Miss Aldriche's formidable presence, Theodora made for the case she had indicated. Apart from the hall, the library was the largest room in the school. It ran to eight good-sized bays of books and, at this time of the day, early evening, gave plenty of choice as to where to sit.

Theodora turned with only mild interest to her grandmother's writings. She would not have chosen to spend time in this way, but Barbara Brighouse had asked her to supper, and Barbara, being a first violin, was not free from rehearsals until six-thirty. The diaries would be a way of passing the time. She piled the heavy leather-bound volumes on the table and prepared to make her way dutifully through them. Surely Grandmother could not have lugged these around the Near East with her? Even in the days of porters they would have been too heavy.

The answer was apparent when she opened the first volume. Disparate individual sheets from a variety of sources had been bound together to preserve them. The later volume, which she had opened first, had letters to and from MPs, and speeches delivered at women's meetings. Then came diaries kept on travels, as Miss Aldriche had said, in Turkey, Egypt and Iran. For someone who had married a priest with a country living her grandmother had gadded about a bit, Theodora thought. She had, of course, her own money, a pleasant small fortune from her Scottish earl father. It all looked moderately affluent and ordinary to Theodora's eyes. As Miss Aldriche had said, Helena Braithwaite had been diligent: labourers' wages had been carefully recorded, as well as the socialising of a vivacious young thing in the twenties; but there was nothing remarkable.

Theodora turned to the other and earlier volume. This was slimmer. It had old school reports at its beginning. St Veep's thick paper recorded Helena MacIntosh's progress in mathematics and French, art and divinity ('Helena should try harder to attend more.') It moved through invitations to dances and a cutting from *The Times* announcing her marriage to the Reverend Henry William Theodore Braithwaite in April 1923, the honeymoon to be spent travelling in Greece.

Idly Theodora turned the pages. Lady Helena's young prose was like having the light, vapid chattering of a wireless in the background. Here were recorded her effusions on seeing the Acropolis by moonlight, there her delight in sailing round Piraeus. Suddenly Theodora's eye was arrested by a sentence. It came apparently from a letter to Helena Braithwaite's mother, an old crone known to Theodora from a single miniature and a great deal of family reminiscence, who had crouched in the family castle in the wilds of Perthshire.

The letter ran: '. . . Dearest Henry has found me the most beautiful wedding present. Well, actually I found it myself in a rather grand shop in Athens, near the Pandemikos Square. It was in the private part at the back. I had wandered in out of the heat because it seemed so dark and cool. It is an annunciation. A painting of St Mary in blue with a silver background. The angel Gabriel on a perfectly gorgeous pair of wings is flying down towards her, pointing his finger at her in a sort of blessing. It is quite small, about two foot six by two foot, painted on board with a rounded top. The frame is quite plain black wood. I keep looking at her and thinking how she must have felt. She looks ageless, but she might have been about my age, do you think? Or is that blasphemous? It is the most perfectly beautiful thing I have ever seen in my whole life. I do hope you will approve it. It seems the perfect picture for a young matron, which is what I now am, you realise, dear Ma. Henry says it's very old, probably as much as five hundred years. He says it may originally have been an icon, a Greek holy picture, which would have been used in worship . . . Only of course that would have been a long time ago. And Henry says it is really not at all Popish. We're going to bring it home in the hand-luggage and I know just where we will hang in at Mark Beech.'

Theodora read the passage again. There were the incidental pleasures of the letter, the naïvety, the girlish care not to alarm a probably Presbyterian mother lodged in the cold north, and none too hospitable perhaps to her daughter's marriage to a well-bred but penniless Anglican priest. But what held Theodora's attention was the description of the icon. Surely it resembled something she had seen and seen recently. Surely the elements described were exactly those she had seen in Jessica's copy, the one she had pressed upon Cromwell just before her abduction.

Theodora turned over the page and there, carefully bound in after the letter, she beheld the beautiful Greek script of an engraved letter-heading which she deciphered to read: Andreas Stephanopoulos, Fine Objects of Antique Art, 12 Pandemikos Square, Athens. Under this was written in western script, 'Icon of the Annunciation; Cypriot, early fifteenth century. Fifteen hundred drachmas.' At the bottom right-hand corner was a faded signature in green ink and the date, 12 April 1923.

CHAPTER TWELVE

Messages

Through the oval porthole of the Turkish airliner, civilisation revealed itself as tiny grey and brown islands in a sea of green fields. As the light began to fade, the Home Counties disappeared slowly beneath the port wing. At the centre of each island, Theodora could just glimpse the tower or spire of a parish church. Such was her concentration, summoned to defend her against the horrendous noise which the Turkish Airlines plane was making, that it was as though she looked out on to silence. The plane's basic seats, bolted imperfectly to the floor, rattled a bit. It looked and felt as though it could be turned over to a military transport at the blink of an eye. It reminded Theodora of some of the flying she'd had to do in Africa.

The intercom crackled and a man's voice announced in Turkish that the aircraft had taken off from Heathrow only one hour late. It continued in English and assured the passengers that food was at hand. They would be landing at Adnan Menderes Airport at 22.00 hours and at Ercam in Northern Cyprus at 03.30. The very thought of it made

Theodora yawn. She leaned back in the rattling seat and reviewed her position.

She and Geoffrey, closeted in the kitchen of her basement flat, had discussed the matter from every angle until far into the night.

'Your theory is,' Geoffrey had said, 'that Dimitri Kostas was able to kidnap Jessica because he looked so like his twin brother, Michel, the Stephanopouloses' driver, that Jessica didn't realise until too late.'

Theodora nodded.

'Where's Michel now?'

'I think he's still with the Stephanopouloses. He has digs in Camden and reports for duty to either the embassy or to Hampstead as he's told.'

'This is according to Stella?' Geoffrey inquired. 'Could you have a word with him?'

'I thought of that. Of course it would be ideal. But on the one hand Stella is not for me asking questions in case it jeopardises Jessica's safety at the hands of the kidnappers. She seems to credit them with supernatural powers, like some sort of mythical Furies.'

'And on the other hand?'

'And on the other hand, of course, I can't question him without an interpreter. My modern Greek just isn't good enough.'

Geoffrey grinned. 'Hexameters not his vernacular?'

'Almost certainly not,' Theodora replied austerely. 'However, I was wondering if you had any information about Dimitri from Mrs Kostas.'

'You remember she came to me on Monday night after her son's death?'

Theodora nodded.

'Well, she told me then she didn't know where her

husband was. I think I mentioned it. What I don't think I mentioned was that on Tuesday morning I went into church to sort out the jumble for the boot sale and I came across the boy, the twin brother, Peter, lurking in the vestry. And he said something curious about his father having said that the fortune of the family had departed. Something like that.'

'Was he referring to the death of his brother?'

'I took it so at the time. But if he did mean that, then that would mean that he was in touch with his father, that his father knew of his son's death, which according to his wife he didn't, or anyway didn't from her. I simply didn't make the connection at the time. And the session with Troutbeck rather pushed it out of my mind.'

'And you didn't manage to catch up with Peter again?'

'No. I charged all over the school looking for him but he'd gone. As I told you, Springer's tale was that his father wanted him with him in Cyprus.'

'So on Wednesday evening you reckon Peter and his father flew to Cyprus?'

'Either that,' Geoffrey agreed, 'or Peter travelled alone and his father had already gone.'

'Do you think they've got Jessica with them?' Theodora asked.

'Wouldn't it be difficult to take a girl out of the country?'

'Not necessarily,' Theodora was authoritative. 'You don't need a passport to go out of Britain, only to get back in. Our regulations are designed to prevent immigration, not emigration.'

'But why should she go willingly?'

'Frightened? Drugged? Compliant for some greater good?'

'Such as?'

'Really,' Theodora gave vent to irritation, 'I don't know. I'm just hypothesising.'

'So if they flew out there need be no check kept by airport authorities?'

'I doubt it. There may be passenger lists if they went out by an airline.'

'Could we check?' Geoffrey clearly felt the need for action.

'We aren't the police. They might not be too willing to tell us.'

'Do you think the police have got this far?' Geoffrey asked.

'I think as far as they're concerned they reckon they've got their man. Ralph Troutbeck's still not been bailed. So why should they look further?'

'I meant,' said Geoffrey, 'as regards Jessica.'

Theodora paused. 'I think there are difficulties about Jessica from the Stephanopoulos end. I've thought from the first they aren't fully cooperating with our police. When I met Stella this morning she as good as admitted as much. She spoke of the husband, George, taking his own steps. She certainly thinks that Jessica's kidnap is a political act to do with George's time in Cyprus before partition. Whether she knows more than that, I'm not sure.'

'So what did George do in Cyprus?'

'Military cultural attaché.'

'Sounds an impossible combination to me,' said the ex-naval officer.

'Culture used as a weapon? It's a bit new to the English scene. But we're getting there. All this heritage stuff is from the same line of country. Using beauty, quality, historic value and worth in order to sell a culture or to dominate one: it's all from the same stable. Like your church, like the portraits at St Veep's, and indeed much else there. We're all in the advertising business now, reinventing tradition like mad.'

'Sad,' said Geoffrey. 'Everything should be itself, and not another thing. However,' he went on, 'I've got a better idea than the police. I know a chap, Harry Gunn. We flew choppers off the *Splendid* together. There's just a chance . . .'

With that Geoffrey gulped the remains of his coffee and flung himself up Theodora's stairs to his own part of the house. Nice of him to think of her phone bill, Theodora reflected.

Twenty minutes later he'd returned, smiling from ear to ear. 'Harry says three seats were booked on Greek Airlines for the 18.40 flight to Larnaca, Southern Cyprus on Wednesday night, in the name of Kostas.'

'Pretty impressive,' Theodora congratulated him. 'Now all we need to know is why?'

'Why?' Geoffrey clearly felt affronted. 'Surely it's enough that they went?'

'Why on earth have the Kostases kidnapped Jessica, if they have, and why was their son killed?' A note of exasperation entered Theodora's voice.

'Are the two connected?'

Theodora felt Geoffrey was being obtuse. 'If the death wasn't an accident, surely they must be. They can't just be coincidental.'

'All right,' said Geoffrey with resignation, 'why?'

'Let's start with the kidnap and leave the killing for a moment.' Theodora was analytical. 'The note to Stella Stephanopoulos said they wanted two icons.'

'Which two?' Geoffrey was not disposed to be helpful.

'Yes, quite. If they wanted the one on Jessica's dressing

table, why not just break in and take it?'

'Perhaps it was the wrong one. Or perhaps they thought Jessica knew where the other was.'

'The only other icon we know about is the one which Jessica gave to Cromwell before she was snatched. And that icon wasn't a copy of the one in her room. The Stephanopoulos one is of a Virgin and child; the Jessica copy one is an annunciation.'

'Where from?' Geoffrey was interested in spite of himself.

'Ah, if only,' said Theodora and then went on. 'Look, there is just a possibility. I had a look at my grandmother's diary in the St Veep's archive this evening. She describes purchasing an icon when she was on her honeymoon in Athens in 1923.' Theodora paused to make quite sure Geoffrey was with her. 'The description which she gives of it matches exactly the one Jessica made a copy of.'

'You don't say,' Geoffrey's response was quite flattering, Theodora felt.

'And what's more, the dealer my grandmother got it from was called Andreas Stephanopoulos.'

'Ha!' said Geoffrey, as triumphant as if he had made the connection himself. 'So where is your grandmother's icon now? Is it amongst her things? Can Jessica have had access to it?'

Theodora shook her head. 'It's not amongst the St Veep's archive, I checked with Miss Aldriche. I can't remember Grandmother having anything which looked like an icon when she was living at Medwich. I won't say I knew every object. I mean, I don't think I ever went into her bedroom, for example. And, of course, by the time I knew her, she was getting on and she'd shed a number of her things round the family, just in order to be able to get into a flat.'

'What happened to her stuff when she died? I mean, apart from the bits that went to St Veep's?'

'Well, I was ten at the time, so I'm not really too sure. But some of it went to my father and some of it to my Great-uncle Hugh, her brother-in-law.'

Geoffrey looked at his watch. It was eleven-twenty. 'Does your uncle keep late hours?'

'All right,' said Theodora with resignation. 'I'll phone him.'

'Use my instrument,' said Geoffrey kindly.

The rattling of the Turkish Airlines' seats seemed to have got louder. Then they began to heave. The man next to Theodora, in a dark suit with a powerful beard waiting to take over his face, suddenly leaned forward, put his head in his hands, and groaned. Theodora glanced across the gangway. Two old women with black dresses and black shawls over their heads had their hands folded, their eyes fixed on the fuselage. Theodora briefly commended her soul to God and resumed her review of events.

The conversation with Canon Hugh had not been easy. It wasn't that he wasn't awake. Though now into his eighties, he kept up a regimen of prayer, reading and gardening which would have sent many a younger man early to bed. But Canon Hugh read his last office at midnight. He had, however – as Theodora knew – his own priorities, from which he was reluctant to depart. Theodora dreaded to intrude upon his routine.

The telephone was answered almost at once. The sound of 'Jesu Joy of Man's Desiring', played on what she recognised as her uncle's flute, was followed by her uncle's voice saying, 'Hugh Braithwaite here, I regret I am not at leisure at the moment. If you wish, you may leave a message after the tone. If, on the other hand, you have inquiries about baptisms, weddings or funerals ...'

Theodora settled down to wait. She should have known that, having discovered the wonders of modern communications. Canon Hugh would use them to the full. 'If, however, you would like to join us at our worship ...'

The tone, when it came at last, was Canon Hugh's flute again, at G-sharp. Theodora winced. 'Uncle Hugh, Theodora here. I'm sorry to butt in on you at this time of night, but I really would like to speak to you rather urgently. I'm phoning from 081 6—.'

'Hello,' Canon Hugh's voice cut in. 'Theodora, my dear, how very nice to hear you.'

The voice conjured up the long bony face, which would have looked well on a horse, and the small, dark study with its view over the fens.

'Where are you?'

'At home. St Sylvester's. I wondered—'

'Are you well?'

'Yes, I'm fine, thank you. And you? Look—'

'I had a touch of rheumatics in my left hand last week which put me back with the tomatoes. But I'm quite recovered now, thank you for your kind inquiry. Have you—'

'Uncle Hugh, I'm sorry to interrupt but I'm ... I haven't too much time. It's about Grandmama's effects.'

'Who?'

'Grandmama Braithwaite, Helena. Your sister-in-law,' she added, lest there should be any mistake.

'Ah, Helena. There was a fine funeral. A bishop, a suffragan, a dean and two canons. Pity your grandfather didn't live to see it.'

'Yes, great pity. What I wanted to know was, what happened to her effects?'

If Canon Hugh found her questions surprising, or even impertinent, he gave no sign. 'The money went three ways: me, your Uncle Louis and your father. May he rest in peace.'

'Yes. Yes. I know. It's not the money. It's the effects.'

'Furniture went to your Aunt Daphne, china to that home for decaying horses, clothes to Oxfam.' Canon Hugh's memory did not apparently fail him. She could almost see him ticking items off on his long, elegant fingers.

'It's the pictures I was interested in. I'm—' She could not stop him. He was off again.

'That appalling Landseer of a cow she was so fond of – I don't know if you recall it? It hung over the drawing-room chimney at Mark Beech and later, when your grandfather got his archdeaconry, in the hall at King's Lynn. That went to . . .' There seemed no way of halting him. He was clearly set to go through the entire collection, their aesthetic merits, their hanging positions in two houses, their ultimate destination.

'Then that portrait of her as a flapper went to her old school, St Veep's.'

'It's that I rather wanted to—'

'I always felt that was its spiritual home. It was a kind of icon of a certain sort of energy, of young womanhood, if you understand me, that sort of thing. It summed up, in a way, some of your grandmother's least admirable qualities.'

'Icons are rather what I wanted to ask about,' Theodora managed to put it. 'I'm trying to trace a particular icon. A Greek or Italian or Cypriot one of an annunciation which Grandmother bought in Greece on her honeymoon in 1923. Hello?' The chatter from Lincolnshire had ceased. There was a marked silence.

'Hello. Uncle Hugh, are you still there?'

'Yes. A Greek icon you say?'

If Theodora could have imagined that it was possible for Canon Hugh to be evasive – and she certainly could – then she would have said that that was what he was being.

'An annunciation,' she pressed him. 'Do you happen to recall it?'

'It was very fine,' the voice seemed more distant, 'very fine indeed. Quite unlike her other stuff. To be honest,' the voice grew more intimate, 'I always coveted it. I had hoped she'd leave it to me.'

'And did she?'

'No,' said Canon Hugh bleakly. 'No, she didn't.'

'So where did it go?'

'It went to the Foxes.'

'Who?'

'Two sisters: Joanna, was it, and Clarissa? Yes, Clarissa; she was the closer of the two.'

'Hell's teeth,' Theodora muttered. 'What is he on about?'

'Helena was at school with them. Then they went into suffrage together. They were cleverer than your grandmother. Girton, I think.' Canon Hugh's voice evinced as much distaste as it was possible for him to reconcile with his priestly profession.

'So when Grandmother died, she left the annunciation to her old friend Clarissa Fox?'

'No, no, she was dead by then. To her daughter, Clarissa: she was at St Veep's too. Regular nest of vipers, St Veep's.'

'I'm doing some part-time teaching there at the moment,' Theodora said.

'Well, I'm sure you do them a great deal of good,' said Canon Hugh heartily. 'Less learning and more religion is what's needed there, by all accounts.'

Theodora wondered whose accounts he'd heard.

'Do you happen to know the name of Clarissa's daughter?'

Canon Hugh's genealogical knowledge did not fail him. 'Bennet,' he said firmly. 'She married Roderick Bennet's second son.'

He's better than a computer, Theodora thought.

Geoffrey and Theodora turned the new knowledge about between them.

If Clarissa Bennet's daughter, Clarissa Two, had been an acquaintance of Jessica's, might that mean that Jessica had had a look at, even been allowed to copy, the Bennet icon, formerly the Braithwaite annunciation? Geoffrey had looked at his watch.

'No,' said Theodora. 'No. I am *not* ringing up a totally unknown parent at a quarter-past midnight to inquire if she has an icon which she allowed a friend of her daughter's to copy.'

'Even if copying it resulted in her abduction?' said Geoffrey. 'Even if it might give an indication of her whereabouts? Even if . . .'

'All right.' Theodora gave in.

Mrs Bennet was the opposite to Canon Hugh in telephone manner. She had a fine line in curtness. Not unnaturally, she was not pleased to be roused and asked the sort of questions which Theodora wanted to put to her. When it got to the crux of the matter, however, she was able to say that yes, she did possess Helena Braithwaite's icon and yes, Jessica had come home with Clarissa on occasions and might well have made a copy of it. Frankly, given how unsuitable her daughter's usual acquaintances were, she'd rather taken to Jessica, who had nice quiet manners and an interest in religion. Surely not a bad thing for young people to have? No, Theodora had hastened to agree with her. And where, Theodora inquired tentatively, where was the icon at the moment? 'Just above my head,' Mrs Bennet replied. 'And since I imagine you're going to ask me to sell it to you, I've had two other offers over the last month – I can save us all a lot of sleeping time by saying I won't.' Theodora heard the sound of a phone being put down.

'Who's asking her to sell, do you suppose?' Geoffrey inquired.

Before she could reply, the phone bell rang. It was Theodora's flat. She answered it.

'Theodora?' The voice was St Veepian. It was Oenone's. 'I'm so sorry to ring you at home at this hour. Except it's just that I can't bear to think of Ralph in that smelly cell.'

Theodora sympathised with her revulsion.

'Well, the reason I'm ringing is that, you remember Geoffrey asked me to have a word with Dame Alicia about Uncle Jeremy's stuff which went to Dick Pound? Dame Alicia said that what he left him was his campaign medals – I really do think it was mean of him not to leave them to Ralph. So marked. I know Ralph's not the military type, but he is his son – and a collection of photographs. It's the photographs I thought might be of interest. You did say icons, didn't you? Yes, well there's a photograph of one.'

'What's it of?' Theodora could not prevent herself from interrupting.

'It's of the Virgin and child. I think. Aren't they all?'

'Not necessarily. What's the setting?'

'Wait a minute. I'll get it.'

'She's enthroned with lots of little angels round her, holding – wait a minute, I'll get a better light – holding a ladder and a mountain in her hand. Would that be rather odd?'

'Not necessarily. Do you happen to know the provenance?'

'On the back it says "Ayia Maria, Montevento, May 1974". Does that help?'

Theodora thought it might.

'Where's Montevento?' Oenone inquired before she rang off.

'Cyprus,' said Theodora. 'Northern, now Turkish Cyprus.'

When she'd gone back to Geoffrey, he'd said gravely, 'It's definitely an icon then, is it, that's caused the death of one child and the kidnap of another?'

'Review the facts,' Theodora invited. 'The Kostas family left Cyprus with an icon. Source, McGrath.'

'If he's reliable.'

'If he's reliable. Dick Pound and Troutbeck have a photograph of an icon, a maesta, by the sound of it, which they took in Cyprus before partition.'

'So the hypothesis is . . .'

'The Kostas brothers brought it out with others and then hung on to it.'

'Why?' Geoffrey asked.

'Perhaps it was too hot to sell because it was well known to art historians. Or maybe because it was especially dear to them, their own personal family's fortune, a sort of talisman. Or, conceivably, it represented their heritage: Greek? Cypriot?'

'Not too much religion there,' Geoffrey ruminated.

'Religion's always mixed up with other things. It's rarely pure. You must have noticed.'

'So then what?'

'Say times changed,' Theodora went on. 'Say the Kostases had to sell and word to this effect got round in the Greek community. Say that became a danger to them. Some other Greek faction thought they ought not to sell or perhaps someone thought they had more right to the sale proceeds than the Kostases.'

'So Kostas père put it in his boy's school holdall for safety?' Geoffrey suddenly recalled the facility with which the two Kostas boys had swapped the black bag between them when he'd met them in the corridor on his way to see Springer on Monday. It must have been within an hour of the boy's death, he realised.

'Our trouble is,' Geoffrey said, 'that we don't know who kept the holdall.'

'It's a fair bet the other twin did, and that's why he and his father decamped to Cyprus.'

'Politically, it's about the right time,' Geoffrey conceded. 'There are new moves afoot to reunite the island.'

'And the Greeks see reuniting as reuniting under Greek, not Turkish sway.'

'So what about Jessica's icon collection?'

'What we know for certain is that – ' Theodora ticked off the information on her fingers – 'one, Jessica had an icon, the Virgin and Child, given her by her grandfather and kept in an icon case in her room. I notice, by the way, that that icon case could be locked. I wonder if Jessica had the key with her when she was taken? However, that's by the way. Two, she had access to another icon, an annunciation, which she made a copy of, which may have been my grandmother's via the Bennet family, which she was showing round the school. Three, she was attending a class at the local Greek Orthodox church to learn how to use icons in prayer. Four, the man who kidnapped her did so without any trouble, which suggests she knew him or thought she did, which would fit if the kidnap driver was the twin brother of her usual driver, Michel Kostas. Five, her father reckons he can manage without the British police and that his daughter's kidnap has something to do with his past career in Cyprus. So . . .'

'So you need to go to Cyprus.'

Theodora stared at him. 'Oh, Geoffrey, I can't.'

'Why not?'

'Well,' said Theodora helplessly, 'It's Lent.'

'I'll tell you what. I'll ring Tim Littlejohn at St George's in Kyrenia. That's Northern Turkish Cyprus of course. You can stay with him and see what you turn up. If it doesn't come to anything, we'll try and interest the police in it.'

The turbulence, Theodora realised had receded. The aircraft's engines were purring more reassuringly. She looked at her watch. It read three in the morning local, Turkish, time. Below her, as she pressed her forehead to the cold glass, were what could only be the lights of Ercan airport. She noticed the man beside her was still asleep. His beard, she noticed, had perceptibly increased.

CHAPTER THIRTEEN

Travels

The Turkish side of the green line – which divides northern Turkish Cyprus from southern Greek Cyprus – is very different from the Greek side. Greek officials are orientated towards tourists. Turks are not. It is, perhaps, the difference between a polis culture and what was for centuries a nomadic one. Pilgrims and wayfarers can be accommodated in the latter, but tourists have different, more degenerate demands, and they can't. The Greeks remain jolly, curious, sanguine and welcoming; the Turks courteous but formal, pessimistic and reluctant.

It took ages to get through customs. Theodora had felt it unfair to descend on the Littlejohns at three in the morning and had, therefore, booked in to the Rotunda in Kyrenia. The hotel, the most modern in the city, when at last reached, had a porter who slept under the reception desk. The Rotunda dated from the thirties and had been built to cater for the end of the British Empire. It had clean thirties lines, green shutters and, by now, lots of peeling plaster. It had a permanent air of ex-patriotism, though the real ex-patriots, finding it too expensive, had moved on to prop up counters in bars buried deep in the sand dunes and tall rushes which fringe the sea-coast area. Bullet holes incurred fifteen years ago at the time of the Turkish invasion made interesting patterns on the entrance-hall walls.

There were compensations, however, for Turkish lack of modernity. The next morning, nothing in the hotel stirred until near eleven. Theodora slept on in her fourth-floor room, while below her the establishment failed to become a hive of activity. Cleaners leant on brooms, waiters and barmen spat on cutlery and glasses to clean off only the greasy bits.

At ten forty-five the electricity came on. There were a great many appliances in the hotel which required electricity, but power was expensive and in short supply, and demanded the sort of mechanical expertise which was in even shorter supply in Turkish culture. So it came on suddenly and went off unpredictably over the whole of the northern part of the island. Its resurgence woke Theodora with a start. The air-conditioning roared. The fridge thundered. A couple of Hoovers, inadvertently left switched on the night before, tuned up outside the door of her room. But the view over Kyrenia bay, when she'd drawn back the shutters, was without spot or stain. Even in April it was warm enough. Pale blue sky met pale blue sea, and to the landward side the curve of the bay showed deep green mountains rearing up near at hand.

Theodora suddenly felt what her grandmother might have felt on her first visit to the Mediterranean, a sense of being off the lead, of things being allowed. The Mediterranean, our second home, Theodora thought, suddenly hopeful of her quixotic enterprise.

She recalled herself to the task in hand. She was not here to enjoy herself, but to find out about a girl kidnapped and a boy dead; to trace, if possible, icons which appeared to be working for evil rather than good. She needed to pray, get some breakfast, and make a plan.

She was surprised to find that the telephone, after only two or three attempts, worked, and the English for coffee and rolls seemed to be within the linguistic capability of whoever was at the other end.

She compromised with the sensuous life so far as to take her office book out on to the verandah. Four hundred yards away, across the bay, under a palm tree, a solitary Turkish soldier stood, rifle in hand, facing the sea. Ready to repel what enemy, Theodora wondered, since the Greek part of Cyprus lay at his back. To the left and right of her, and below but not above – since she was on the top floor – were ranged the verandahs of the other rooms. One by one, shutters rattled and creaked open and guests emerged. Some stayed, others snuffed the air and then retired, like lizards into a wall.

There was constant sudden or cautious movement. The man immediately to Theodora's right, wrapped in an enormous plum-coloured bathrobe, scraped his table into place to receive his coffee tray. For an instant he turned his face towards her and, behind the dark glasses, she recognised the beard growth of her plane travelling companion of last night. The smell of his coffee drifted tantalisingly towards her. She could do with some of that right now.

The telephone, when it shrilled, startled her. At the same moment there was a knock on her door. The small, dark-haired maid held a tray smilingly towards her. Theodora indicated the fridge as a possible surface, and reached for the phone. As she did so, she heard a scream. The maid lay on the floor, clutching her hand. The tray swayed at a precarious angle on top of the fridge.

'Just a minute,' Theodora said into the phone, and dashed towards the maid. She reached out to steady the tray and prevent it from falling. The maid cried out again, knocking Theodora's hand away from the metal handles. 'Yok. Forbid touch. It is the electrics.'

Where have I heard that before? Theodora asked herself. She helped the still trembling girl towards the bed and reached cautiously for the phone.

'Hello,' said an anxious English voice. 'Is that Miss Braithwaite? This is Tim Littlejohn. What's happening?'

Theodora took a grip on herself. She wasn't sure what was happening, so best to play it down.

'There's been a slight accident with the electricity here. It seems to run wild rather and attack the innocent. One of the maids received a bit of a shock. I think she's going to recover.'

She glanced at the girl, whose crying had subsided.

'We're not too reliable in that quarter,' said Mr Little-john apologetically. 'I'll be down in twenty minutes and we'll sort something out.'

'I really don't know,' Theodora replied in answer to Tim Littlejohn's question. 'You see, the Kostas boy was killed by being thrown, the police think deliberately, against an electrical unit.'

'So you said. On the other hand, as I said, I have to admit electricity isn't one of the Turk's things. Don't mistake me,' the Anglican priest continued, 'the Turks are a very good sort of people.' He thought for a moment. 'They're very good soldiers. Give them an order and they do it to the letter, until they're told to stop.' He paused again. 'It has its disadvantages, of course, too.'

'Like my soldier under the palm tree,' Theodora said. 'He looked very much as though he'd been given an order long ago and then been forgotten.'

'Not impossible.' Tim swung the four-wheel-drive Suzuki over the pot-holes in the main road at a good speed. He was a small whippet of a man in a faded blue Airtex shirt and grey flannels. He could not have been other than English. He perched on the high seat and handled the steering wheel, which looked too large for him, with great skill. The colours of the country were light yellow roads, light green herbage scattered with pink and yellow flowers, and dark green and grey mountains as a backdrop. As they left the suburbs of Kyrenia behind and noon approached, it got warmer.

'Going to be hot?' Theodora inquired.

'Not really by our standards, but I expect it'll feel so if you're fresh from the Home Counties. Look,' he added, turning to glance at her. 'Geoffrey rang last night. He filled me in on the rough outline. I really think it would be better if you stayed with me and Gwyneth at the vicarage. In view of the electrics.'

'It's very kind. I'd love to if you don't mind. Hotels are not really my thing. And if I'm going to have to watch it every time I see a socket, it's going to be a bore.'

'That's settled then. The next thing is the plan of action. We need to find Jessica and the icon or icons. Right?'

'Right.'

'And the Kostases will have entered through Larnaca airport – the Greek side – since the Turks don't let any Greeks in on this side.'

Theodora nodded.

'But the Kostases' original village was here in the Turkish bit, at Montevento?'

'So McGrath said.'

'Is he trustworthy?'

'Oh, I should think so in something like that. It could so easily be checked.'

'Why do you suppose they've brought Jessica here – if she *was* the third person on the flight?'

'One reason might be that they want to keep her out of someone else's hands.'

'You reckon there are a number of people, all after an icon or icons?'

'It looks like it.'

'Why?'

'They have more than religious significance, don't they? I mean, they can become political symbols as well.'

'Too true. Think of that Polish madonna thing.' The Reverend Tim's voice suggested distaste. 'It's amazing what people think religious art can be used for.'

Here Theodora could agree with him. 'I've always thought hanging religious pictures in galleries is as bad as selling them for cash or using them for politics.'

'I'm sure you're right,' Tim said distantly. 'I think myself that we're better off without them in Christianity.'

Theodora felt this was a perfectly respectable view. She just did not happen to share it. She had, however, no intention of arguing the point with her kind host.

'And reunification's in the air?' Theodora pursued.

'When isn't it? We pray daily for it. But it can't happen with present attitudes. You saw the soldier.'

'But if someone thought there might be a possibility of uniting the island again, and wanted a symbol round which to unite interests?'

'Greek interests, not Turkish, you mean?'

'Greek interests, of course. Then couldn't an icon serve the purpose?'

Tim looked dubious. 'You might be right. I wouldn't pretend to understand the Greek mentality any more than the Turkish.' He changed gear to deal with a tricky concatenation of pot-holes.

'The parish is mostly an expatriate one then; you don't aim to bring in from outside?' Theodora gestured in the direction of the countryside in general to indicate what she took to be Tim's patch.

'Turkish law, which more or less prevails here, allows, in practice, freedom of worship but no proselytising. For example, I'm not supposed to wear clerical dress outside the church building. The Greek Orthodox Church is bound by the same limitations, but actually it gets a worse deal than us. Their buildings were closed down after partition. Later a lot of them were ransacked. The Turks really didn't behave at all well. A fair amount of stuff has seeped out on to the international art market from here, I believe.'

'What about the monasteries: how did they fare?'

'If they were fairly remote, had no more than a few old monks and nothing of value and kept their heads down, they got by. Now, of course, the Turks want (a) tourism and (b) the Common Market, so they're treading more carefully.' There was a pause as Tim renegotiated his way past a couple of coaches of German tourists.

'So how many do you get in St George's?'

'Our average Sunday turn-out,' said Tim modestly, 'is about eighty at matins. We can double that at the festivals.'

'The expatriate community is highly Christianised?'

'Well, honesty compels me to say that it's partly a social matter. We're all middle aged to old. We're mostly middle class, too, retired colonial service or armed services, where the C of E is part of the deal. People who've lived in warm climates since their twenties aren't going to go back to

Surbiton any more. The drink's cheap and, as I say, the Turks are no trouble to us. But there's a real commitment as well. Lots of sound Christian charity. Anyway,' Tim was defensive, 'they need God as well as the next person, and I'm happy to serve.' He pushed the accelerator down to make his point.

Theodora hadn't wished to suggest otherwise, and turned the conversation back to the matter in hand. 'So how could one go about learning whether there's anything stirring politically?'

'You mean whether anyone has come across the green line? It's a very risky thing to do. The Turks brought in their own people after the invasion. And they literally set up in the houses of the Greeks they'd pushed out. I remember going down to Kyrenia to try and make contact with some Greek friends of ours soon after the takeover. I knocked at the door and there was an entire Turkish family eating off the very dinner plates on the very table our friends had left behind.' The Reverend Tim Littlejohn stamped on the brake, cornering with passion at the memory.

'You could see it would make for enmity.' Theodora rocked back in her seat as they gathered speed again.

'You can say that again.' He pushed the accelerator in compensation.

'So is there any way of getting information?'

Tim changed gear to accommodate the sudden appearance of a shingle road surface, then braked suddenly. From the ditches on either side of the road rose up a dozen men in army fatigues. They had rifles trailing from their hands. They wore blue berets and had fair hair. Their leader stepped into the middle of the road and waved them down. He put his head into the driver's side and said in excellent

Swedish-accented English, 'I can warn you the road in front is dangerous because there is a big fall of rocks.'

'Yes,' said Tim cheerfully. 'Thanks very much for telling me. Actually I did come down that way an hour ago, so I expect I'll be all right.'

'The United Nations train here,' he said conversationally to Theodora as he got up speed again.

'So I see.'

'We always have fish on Friday in Lent, just to remind us,' said Mrs Littlejohn, pushing the tomato sauce bottle towards Theodora. The flabby, tough, battered fish and the limp, large, greasy chips didn't quite fit the house, which was general-issue Mediterranean modern villa. But it did fit the décor which was chintz and welsh dressers and it did fit Gwyneth Littlejohn's accent which was Welsh too.

Theodora had really only one thought in her mind. She resumed where the United Nations had interrupted. 'If anything unusual was happening, who would know? I'm thinking about Jessica.'

'That poor girl. How can people be so wicked,' said Gwyneth. 'Will they never rest from playing soldiers?'

'I've been thinking of that,' said Tim, evidently replying to Theodora rather than his wife. 'The best bet is probably the Vounikis at the Paradise Garden.'

Theodora glanced across at him. 'We've got a Paradise Garden in Betterhouse. It's a good restaurant,' she added, looking at the remains of the fish on her plate.

'So is ours. Vouniki's got a good little corner there. If we dined there we might pick up something. Vouniki's is a centre of gossip. I've noticed the old man knows what's happening in the docks, and he's well informed about border crossers.'

'So they do cross the border?'

'There's a black market here as well as in most places.'

Mrs Littlejohn produced rice pudding and strawberry jam.

'If we're going to eat at the Paradise, we ought to save ourselves,' she said, ladling out very small quantities of rice into the willow-pattern dishes. Theodora hoped that the Cyprus version of the Paradise Garden was as good as the Betterhouse one.

'How good is your Turkish?' Theodora ventured. If they were to make progress, they would need to be assured in that area.

'He's very good,' said Gwyneth with pride. 'He's been taking lessons.'

'Well, I'm serviceable, I think. I can certainly pick up whether a family of Greeks called Kostas have infiltrated the border clasping an icon in either hand and with a young English girl in tow. If they'll talk, that is. Did Geoffrey . . .?' Tim approached a delicate subject delicately.

'He suggested a certain amount of sterling.'

'You've got it with you?'

'Do you want it?'

'Keep it until required.'

The Reverend Littlejohn seemed to think the business side of things was at an end. He leaned back in his chair and discarded his napkin. 'We do follow the local custom of the siesta.' He glanced meaningfully at the china cottage on the mantelpiece, in the middle of which could be seen a clock face.

The vicarage's guest room was filled with early afternoon light. Theodora lifted the jalousies and gazed up at the mountain, grey and sheer, about fifty kilometres away. The lower slopes were covered with dark pines, the upper were bare rock. With difficulty she discerned first the monastery and then, perched above it, the castle. They were so much part of the stone that they looked more like natural features than the work of human hands. Military and religious power had, after a thousand years, merged into one harmonious whole with the natural world.

She ought to have been tired after the flight and exertions of the journey. But she could not settle. The bookcase was the usual set of guests' leavings and family cast-offs. There were two or three ancient crime novels: *Clerical Errors, Unholy Ghosts.* Tim's geography textbooks, and something entitled *Travels in the Isle of Cyprus* by the Reverend Canon J. F. Hetherington-Pollock, published privately in a limited edition with steel engravings in 1925. Just the job, thought Theodora. If that didn't send her to sleep, nothing would. Idly she turned the thick pages, dipping here and there into the canon's description of castles and monasteries, his disquisitions, on the etymology of place names and his remarks on the bird population and flora. Her eyelids were beginning to droop when she came to the chapter called 'History and Legend' and read:

On 1 May 1425, a Venetian mercenary captain, Giovanni Dionisotti, threw his Greek wife, Maria, off the battlements of the castle of Montevento in northern Cyprus. When he discovered that she was innocent of the adultery of which he had accused her, he spent a considerable part of his ample fortune on commissioning what came to be known as the Venetian Triptych. This splendid work depicted an annunciation and a madonna with child flanking a maesta. This the repentant soldier lodged in the tiny Greek

Orthodox church of Ayia Maria in the village of Montevento at the foot of the castle.

The work, which was generally admitted to be of the highest quality, was, despite its Italian origins and style, taken to the hearts of the local Cypriots. For five hundred years it served the worshippers of that country as a window into the heavenly order, receiving their prayers and petitions, working its modest quota of miracles. But in the early morning of 1 May 1920 the area round the church was shaken by the tremors attending a minor earthquake, and when the church was inspected the triptych was gone. A thorough search was made far and near, for not only was the honour of the village at stake, but so also was its prosperity. The withdrawal of the image was felt as keenly as would be the withdrawal of the patronage of heaven itself. How could the village flourish if the Mother of God had left it? The villagers felt themselves to be accursed. And so it proved. The triptych failed to come to light and a series of disasters rendered the village a desolation within a decade.

Theodora raised her head. So that was it. The Venetian Triptych was what they were all after: the Kostases, who regarded it as an object of superstition, as indeed their own personal luck, or who perhaps saw that luck in concrete terms of dollars; the Greek Cypriot government, who would like to be able to use it as a focus for nationalistic feeling; the Turks, who would be concerned to prevent either of those courses.

How had each of the three icons been dispersed? Had the original theft after the earthquake been perpetrated by the Kostases, or had they come by it later? Had they kept the maesta, the crowning glory of the piece, and sold the other two panels to the Stephanopouloses? And had that family in time sold the annunciation to Lady Helena in 1924 in Athens, and passed the other to Jessica in due course in the 1980s? How had Troutbeck and Pound been able to photograph the maesta in Cyprus in '74?

And what was going to happen now? Who had which icons with what intentions, and why had one boy been killed and a girl kidnapped? Theodora thought of the note which Stella Stephanopoulos had received. It suggested that one party at least had the idea that Jessica had access to two of the icons, presumably the Virgin and child, which was her own from her grandfather, and the annunciation, originally Helena's. Well, thought Theodora as she lay back on the Littlejohns' covers and closed her eyes, perhaps this evening will reveal more.

Geoffrey lay back on his bed and gazed at the ceiling. It was cracked and he found himself tracing the coast of Cyprus in its crazy lines. He clasped his hands behind his head and flapped his elbows a couple of times. He felt full of energy; he ought to find someone to play squash with. Thursday was his day off. He'd driven Theo to Gatwick at six and now at eight-thirty he didn't know what to do with himself. He wondered if he'd been right to wave Theo off on her flight to Cyprus. Something, he felt in his bones, was due to happen there, but still there were gaps. If Theo was going to track down Jessica and deal with the Stephanopoulos side of things, the least he could do was to follow up the Kostas affair in Betterhouse.

Someone in Betterhouse had killed young Kostas. They had killed, Theodora and he had agreed, to get their hands on an icon. Who would kill for such an end, and how had

187

they done it? Geoffrey shook his head. He didn't want to
play detective. He was a priest not a policeman. His own
concerns were pastoral. He could look to and help to
assuage the grief of Mrs Kostas at the death of her son.
He knew how to do that. He could sympathise and support
the maladroit young Troutbeck in prison and, if need be,
through a trial. He knew how to do that too. In all else he
had resolved he would be no more than a spectator. His
training both as a naval officer and as a priest had taught
him that nothing is achieved without prioritising. Set your
goals and make them achievable, his spiritual director
always told him, and leave the rest to God, otherwise you'll
dissipate your energies and do more harm than good. And
he quite agreed with that. But still someone had killed
Kostas and he couldn't help feeling that if he thought hard
enough he could put his finger on them. He had enough
information, it was just a matter of bringing the bits
together.

Could it really have been Troutbeck? His father had
known young Kostas's father and had known, certainly
known about (if Oenone's photograph meant anything) the
provenance of an icon. What was it McGrath had said?
'Who drove the Greeks out of Cyprus? The Turks.' But
Geoffrey didn't know of any Turks in Betterhouse. And
when he had at last caught up with Springer in the school
dining hall, he'd affirmed he didn't know any either. 'How
about your database?' Geoffrey had urged. They had
watched the green script scroll down the screen, first under
'ethnic origin' then under 'religion'. Neither category yiel-
ded up any Turkish pupils.

'Why did you want to know, Geoff?' Springer had asked.
'Just a hunch about Kostas's killer,' Geoffrey had replied.
Springer shook his head sagely and laid his hand on

Geoffrey's arm as though to comfort one who cannot face the truth unsupported. 'I think we know, Geoff, don't we, you and me, that young Troutbeck just wasn't up to things. He wasn't a fully mature and integrated personality, and you've just got to be all that and, yes, more, in today's education context. It's not just demanding, it's not just challenging, it's a—'

Geoffrey had freed himself from Springer's grip and plunged down the concrete stairs. Now, eight hours later, he looked at his watch and wondered if Springer was right. McGrath had said Troutbeck wasn't up to it, wasn't the man his father was. Geoffrey had wondered if he should try and see McGrath again, but when he'd inquired for him he was told he'd taken a day's leave. What had he meant by Turks? Perhaps, Geoffrey told himself with a sigh, there really was nothing he could do. He sprang off the bed and made for the kitchen. Food would be sensible.

Competent though he was in many spheres, Geoffrey was no cook. He didn't like to admit it, but recently he'd come to rely on Theodora providing sustenance at least to the level of the odd bacon sandwich. With her away, he didn't fancy his own larder. Paradise Garden would be the best bet at this time of night.

Outside the vicarage, it was raining steadily. He marched swiftly past the church which loomed up at him out of the spring darkness, and strode past the retreat house of St Sylvester. He wondered briefly if Gilbert Racy might be free. Then he decided he wasn't up to Gilbert's mixture of scholarship and gossip, and instead pressed on down towards the high street.

He almost missed the entrance to the restaurant. The flashing sign with its red neon palm tree and fountain in green and blue was dark. But when he pushed open the door and edged inside, all was as usual. Harry hurried forward to take his umbrella; a couple of the younger editions were instantly at hand to conduct him to his usual table next to the bar and produce a menu.

'What's up with your sign, Harry?' Geoffrey asked when he had ordered the usual.

'Ah, Reverend Geoffrey,' Harry wrung his hands in theatrical anguish, 'we have such trouble. First the palm tree does not light, and now it is the fountain and bowl. The bowl works but not the water, then the water and not the bowl. Now all are gone, dark.'

'Trade affected?'

'I think I shall survive, but it looks bad. Without the sign it looks like we do not welcome our customers.'

'Oh, I don't think anyone would think that,' Geoffrey assured him, looking round for the bartender. The usual man wasn't on, but a young apprentice materialised rapidly, eager to meet his wishes.

Harry brightened. 'They come, the electrics, they promised they come this morning. Now they phone me and it will be tonight. We shall see.' He was grim. 'My cousin, the electric, he is very busy, he says.'

'Hasn't affected the cooking, I hope.'

Harry was scandalised. 'The reverend gentleman knows we do everything on charcoal.' Then he went on delicately, 'Your colleague, she will be joining you perhaps later?'

'Oenone? Oh, Theo. No, she's taking a holiday.'

'Ah, a spring holiday. How very delightful. Somewhere healthy perhaps?'

'Cyprus,' said Geoffrey, who felt he'd had enough of this desultory conversation and wanted his kid.

'That is a very beautiful and very healthy place,' Harry declared.

'You know it?' Geoffrey was polite.

'Of course, in my youth—' Harry began. But he was interrupted by the arrival of Geoffrey's food. At the same time the street door opened and yet another Harry looka-like stood on the threshold, a metal tool-carrier in his hand. Harry flicked his napkin and hurried to greet the electric cousin.

Geoffrey murmured his grace and then tried and failed to eat slowly. Eight years at boarding school, followed by twelve years in the navy, had formed his eating habits irredeemably. In record time he pushed the last piece of pitta round his plate and raised it to his lips. As he did so the lights in the dining room went out. There was, however, no kerfuffle. The candle on his table was augmented almost without pause by an oil lamp placed by an invisible hand. Harry could be heard giving orders in the back kitchen. The two other tables which were occupied were similarly served. It was time, Geoffrey felt, to leave them to their troubles.

'The electrics, they have come,' Harry said as he handed Geoffrey his umbrella at the door.

'That's good, then,' Geoffrey answered as he stepped out into the night. Outside, by the kerb and under the street-lamp, a battered-looking Bedford van with its back door open revealed a mass of cables and copper wire. Geoffrey glanced at the side. On it was painted 'Smith and Vouniki, Electricians, Installations and Maintenance'.

'Good Lord,' said Geoffrey, who was never profane. He swung on his heel and turned rapidly back towards the already closing door of the restaurant. Harry was convers-ing loudly with the electrician. 'Yok,' he was saying 'Yok, yok, yok.'

'Oh heck,' said Geoffrey. Of course, he thought, *Turkish*

Cypriots. And – he made the final connection – the contractors' board outside South West London Comprehensive School showed just where these Turkish electricians had been operating recently.

The prevalent impression was of cats. Large ones quartered the dining room territorially between them. Smaller ones scudded in and out through the open doors. Waiting cats perched on the wall of the tiny courtyard, lurking ones slid in and out from the lee of old kerosene drums which, painted white, held either geraniums or electric lamps. It wasn't quite warm enough to sit out once the sun had gone down, but Vouniki's large, kitchen-like dining room had its door and windows open on to the garden.

Theodora found it a most sympathetic ambience. There was a more leisured pace than at the Paradise Garden in Betterhouse, a more scholarly and negotiated approach to the choosing of food, but it sounded familiar when the Reverend Tim Littlejohn leaned over the menu towards her and said, 'The choice of meat is more apparent than real. It may say chicken or rabbit or whatever but in fact it's always—'

'Kid,' said Theodora.

'And always—' said Mrs Littlejohn.

'Delicious,' said Theodora.

Tim disappeared into the kitchen to order, talk and listen. He returned, clearly pleased with himself. 'Vouniki père isn't here at the moment, but he's expected soon. Also, they expect someone from the port who has news from the Greek side. He'll be here soon. So really that's about as good as we could hope for in the circs.'

Theodora agreed. She wondered whether to share her researches about the Venetian icon with the Littlejohns and decided against it for the moment.

They had come early. Service was leisurely. Gradually the rest of the tables began to fill up. English was heard, German was heard, Turkish was heard. Paradise Gardens were clearly as popular in Cyprus as they were in Better-house. Rightly so, thought Theodora, as she attacked her kid.

Conversation was naturally of 'home', of England. Gwyneth Littlejohn evinced an interest in the doings of the royal family which Theodora was unable to satisfy. Tim would have liked to explore church politics, including women's ordination, but felt constrained by not knowing Theodora's views and settled safely for a run through common acquaintances.

At nine-fifteen sharp all the lights went out. There was no perceptible increase in noise. Nobody, indeed, raised an eyebrow. There was an interval of a couple of minutes. When the waiter brought the kerosene lamp and removed their plates, a long brown envelope had appeared in the shadow of the wine bottle. This was the response, Tim intimated, to his inquiries in the kitchen, though there was no name on it. Tim opened it and read it. Then he translated from the Turkish for the benefit of his womenfolk.

'Greek Major Stephanopoulos arrived yesterday evening at Larnica airport to attend a conference on reunification. Greek-Briton staying in Nicosia intends crossing the border as a pilgrim tomorrow and going to Montevento'.

'So what's Stephanopoulos doing here, would you suppose?' Gwyneth asked.

'Why not take him at his word and accept that he's come to the conference, and also presumably to see if he can hear word of Jessica?'

'How would he know she's here?'

'Perhaps,' Theodora answered, 'he did what we did and rang the airline to see who was going out on Greek flights. His wife seemed to think he was taking his own measures and not relying on the English police.'

'And how about the "Greek-Briton"? Who would that be and what would he be doing coming from the Greek side to the Turkish for a pilgrimage to Montevento?' Gwyneth tried again.

'If he were Greek, the Turks wouldn't let him in this side: he'd have to start from the Greek.'

'Would that mean a Kostas?' Gwyneth inquired.

'Well, perhaps,' Theodora answered. 'Though I'm not too sure about their devoutness. But of course their village is St Mary's at Montevento. Anyway, it looks as if I ought to go to Montevento and see what's brewing.'

Gwyneth Littlejohn put her napkin down and leaned forward. She looked deep into Theodora's eyes, as though she were about to read her fortune. Her thick dark bobbed hair swung round her cheeks and she said, her Welsh accent strengthening, 'I'd really very strongly urge you to be careful. Cyprus isn't like England. You can get killed very much more easily.'

Theodora wondered when they'd last lived in England. It seemed to her that Betterhouse was also an easy place to get killed in. However, she recognised the kindness of her hostess's intentions.

'I'm sure all will be well, Gwyneth. My guess is that there's going to be some icon swapping at Montevento, and if that means I can get news of Jessica, then I think I should go.'

'Why don't you tell the police, Tim?' Gwyneth Littlejohn turned to her husband.

'Oh, come on, dearie, you know what they're like here.

Unless they're heavily bribed and indeed unless they suspect a crime is an offence under their law, they aren't going to stir a stump. Anyway, it's not clear that anything criminal except a border-crossing is going on, and that's not a crime in my book.'

Gwyneth Littlejohn supposed he was right. 'However,' she said firmly to Theodora', 'you can't go alone, my dear.' She laid a hand on Theodora's. 'And Tim can't take you tomorrow; he's got sick communions and then a PCC. I'll drive you.'

Theodora folded the map over her knee and Gwyneth Littlejohn drove. The map was worse than useless since it marked only the Greek names of villages, and one of the few tasks which the Turks had performed thoroughly was that of changing the signposts and village nameboards from Greek to unrelated Turkish names. Hence, though Theodora had been aghast at the idea of Gwyneth Littlejohn coming with her, she had to admit she knew what she was about and she was grateful.

They'd set off at dawn and made good speed over the track towards the mountains. The sun came up as the pine forest dwindled and they reached the rocky, single-track road which would bring them eventually to Montevento. On the map and from the windows of the Littlejohns' guest room it had all looked quite near and possible. As they approached, the reality, however, was different. The road was steep and deeply rutted with rockfalls precipitated by the winter rains. Hairpin bend followed hairpin bend monotonously. Progress was slow.

'How would someone crossing the border get up here?'

'There's more than one way up. Coming from Kyrenia this is the fastest way. Coming from Nicosia there're two ways, and they both come round the back.'

'Are there tourists?'

'Oh, yes. Increasingly. At first the Turks were very suspicious of anyone. Now they're still suspicious, but they want the currency and the good name. It doesn't mean they put labels on things or offer the odd signpost, in any other language. But they don't actually gun you down if you want to get to a site of historical interest.'

Theodora wasn't sure how reassured she was by this.

'The Germans,' Gwyneth prattled on, 'have done a lot to help really. The Turks trust them from the '14–'18 war, of course. And the Germans are great cultural travellers. Very pushy, very well informed and determined.'

Gwyneth completed the blind corner and stamped on her brakes. The back of the coach said in gothic letters. 'Gottfried Hellman, Kultural Tourischen, Heidelberg'.

'See what I mean?' said Gwyneth in triumph. 'Still, we can fall in behind him and let him do the work.'

An hour and a half later, at eleven-thirty, they turned yet one more corner and came out on to a plateau, brownish green in colour from a strong growth of ryegrass. They found themselves looking down on the monastery which had been built in a dip in the hills, and gazing up at the castle perched behind. There were no other vehicles apart from themselves and the coachload of Germans. The monastery's small dome and single block of cells looked toylike in the distance. There was utter silence. Then the door of the coach was flung open and a babble of German filled the air. Theodora watched them descend. Most were middle aged, many of the men wore hats and all wore raincoats. Amongst the last to edge down the high steps was a figure faintly familiar to her: for a moment when he turned his face towards her she recognised her ill-shaved friend from the plane and hotel.

'What do you want to do?' asked Gwyneth.

Theodora turned her gaze towards the castle which looked, doubtless misleadingly, about a mile away.

'I don't think I want to mix it with the German party in the monastery. I wonder if it would be a good idea if I went and cased the castle while you stay here and keep an eye open for new arrivals?'

'Right you are,' said Gwyneth. 'What are we looking for?'

'Well, certainly a Kostas or a Stephanopoulos, and then anyone who contacts them.'

'Were you a Guide?' asked Gwyneth unexpectedly.

Theodora admitted she had been a patrol leader. Gwyneth Littlejohn nodded. 'I thought I recognised a fellow Guide. I was commissioner for Llandryneth for nearly fourteen years before I met Tim. And I don't think the skill has deserted me.'

She suddenly clutched her person about knee level and plunged both hands deep into a concealed trouser pocket. From it she produced two large red handkerchiefs and sprang to attention with the pieces of cloth clasped in front of her.

'Ready to transmit message,' said Theodora suavely.

'Off you go,' said Gwyneth. 'And don't take any more risks than you need.'

Theodora started the climb in good fettle, but a hundred yards up, the steep, irregular steps found her sweating and panting. Life in Betterhouse had made her soft. Have to do some regular exercise when I get back – *if* I get back – she resolved. Halfway up she stopped and looked down. The German party were in an orderly file nearing the monastery. The Suzuki and Gwyneth were parked under the one tree some distance away. Far to the right, Theodora thought she glimpsed a glint, as of sun on the windscreen of a miniature car, its grey form scarcely discernible against the rock, appearing and disappearing round the circuitous track.

She turned once more to her task. The stairs gave out and the steps became simple footholds cut into the living rock. She was still nowhere near the castle entrance. She looked up at it and, with an experienced eye, took in the curtain wall and the enceinte. The entrance was a single round arch with the remains of one tower. Leading off from either side were battlements crumbling back into mountain rock. Behind them the second set of walls looked in better condition. Eleventh century with thirteenth-century additions, she thought as she caught sight of the chapel and vaulted hall. Clumps of valerian and small ferns fringed and softened the unmortared masonry; in and out of the crevices lizards scuttled and rustled.

There was no nonsense about signs telling visitors to beware of fallen masonry, of which there was a considerable amount on the ground. The ministry of works was conspicuous by its absence; poor access for the disabled, too, Theodora thought, swinging herself over the insecure piles towards the inner wall.

Here officialdom had belatedly caught up. An irregularly painted notice, much blistered and peeling off, offered in Turkish and English museum, chapel and bar. All human needs, Theodora thought with scepticism, and made for the final set of steps which let to the battlements of the inner walls.

At the top she found a broad paved walk running between the machicolations. The sun-warmed stones invited. She selected an embrasure and sat down. The silence was absolute, except for a raven cawing somewhere below her. The view through the slit was like a miniature in a manuscript, toy mountains in the distance, red poppies near at hand and below, oh heavens, the red flash of Gwyneth embarking on a semaphore message.

Theodora focused her field glasses and Gwyneth sprang into view. She picked out the letters with difficulty and read: 'English priest in car.' Who on earth? For a moment she wondered if Geoffrey had by some chance arrived. Gwyneth was still signalling. 'Has parcel, entering castle.' Theodora read the 'end of message' sign and looked down towards the entrance. Because the battlements curved and the entrance tower was well set in, it was difficult to see whether any one was entering. She began to walk slowly round the battlements, leaning out over them every twenty yards to see if visibility had improved.

At the third attempt she was dismayed to see half a dozen mackintoshed figures filing through the archgate. The German party had completed their visit to the monastery in record time. She scrutinised each, but could see no one whom she could identify by the description of 'British priest with a parcel'. Not one of them looked like an Anglican.

She looked back to where she had last seen Gwyneth, but of her there was now no sign. Perhaps she had better descend and check the German crowd as they moved towards the keep, as they surely must do. Germans would want to see the museum and the chapel. They'd know about vaulting. If she didn't hurry she'd miss them. She began the descent, carefully measuring and placing her steps on each worn stair. She seemed to have got a second wind, or else the descent was easier. At the bottom she met a figure picking its way daintily over the fallen masonry and holding a sunshade aloft. The woman glanced at Theodora and said with a smile and in excellent English, 'It is amazing what we do in the name of culture, isn't it?' Theodora wished she felt she could have answered in as good German, and wondered with regret whether she really looked as English as all that.

At the bottom of the stair it was possible to command the whole of the approach from the entrance arch. No one of the remainder of the party looked like an English priest. Hell's teeth, had she come all this way only to miss her quarry? Where was he? What was going on? She tossed up between the chapel and the bar. Where, after all, would you negotiate a deal? She struck off towards the bar, not really believing in its existence in this remote place. It would presumably be a roofed building. She spotted a roof at the far end of the battlement. Once more she raced up the stairs and jogged round the broad path. At the far end there was a door which looked as though it had not been opened in many years. From the other side came the sound of music. Cautiously she turned the handle. Four interested male faces turned towards her. They were seated at a well-appointed bar with glasses in front of them. Abruptly the music ceased and a voice said, 'This is the BBC World Service.'

I think I've had enough of surprises, Theodora thought. She ordered an orange juice and took it out on to the minuscule balcony. All I want is an English priest carrying a parcel. All I get is Germans hunting culture and Turks improving their English. She sipped her juice disconsolately. Far away in the distance she could see the tiny monastery and, walking purposefully towards it, a black figure. She downed the juice and set off at a pace which would have pleased the former Guide commissioner for Llandryneth.

At the door of the monastery chapel she paused, drew breath, and then edged inside. It was dark and smelt of incense and damp. It would have held no more than a dozen people, she estimated, and at the moment it was quite empty. To the left of the iconostasis was a door in the wall. She crossed quickly towards it. It was ajar. She pulled it open and stepped out into a tiny, sunlit court, in the middle of which was a well-head, an almond tree, and two figures on a stone bench, seated slightly apart. One of the figures was familiar: a heavy-looking man with a growth of beard. The other was slight and younger and, to Theodora's eye, unmistakably English. Between them lay a parcel.

'Kallistos Bury,' said Theodora firmly, 'where is Jessica Stephanopoulos?'

CHAPTER FOURTEEN

Celebrations

'This is Sir Solomon Piatigorsky,' said Dame Alicia with pride. There was a general murmur of well-bred applause. The party in the first mistress's lodgings after St Veep's Lent concert was always a select affair. The parents of pupils who had performed were invited, together with anyone else Dame Alicia felt would add lustre to the occasion. Admiral Topglass of the US navy, Mrs Bennet, a governor of the BBC, Sir Nicholas Hapgood from the Treasury, had all merited invitations. Theodora reckoned she'd been invited to be paraded before the ecclesiastical governors to show she was presentable. The bishop had been approving, 'Of course, I knew your dear father.' The canon of Exeter had been jocular, 'Stretches you a bit, coping with our youngsters, I expect,' he'd said, his hand comfortably round a glass.

Geoffrey had been invited because Oenone had wanted him, and Dame Alicia was very relieved to have the Stephanopoulos muddle sorted out without its having hit the press, and was therefore disposed to meet Oenone's requests in case she might be tempted to spill the beans. Not, she thought, that she didn't trust Miss Troutbeck, but there had been unsavoury gossip about her brother. He'd just been released from police questioning about the murder of one of his pupils. She hadn't inquired because obviously there must have been a mistake. The Troutbecks were a perfectly pukka family. She'd looked them up and Anne Aldriche had vouched for them. But it was as well to be on the safe side.

Cromwell oozed over to Theodora to rescue her from the canon. 'You saw *The Times*?' he inquired of the grateful Theodora.

'To be honest, I wrote it.'

'The safest way in specialist matters.'

A muted paragraph had recorded the remarkable fact that the art world had recently been delighted by the reuniting of the famous Venetian Triptych, a set of three icons painted in Cyprus in the fourteenth century by an Italian master, the whereabouts of which had been uncertain since they disappeared from Ayia Maria, Montevento, Cyprus in the 1920s. It appeared that the three panels were now in the hands of the Greek Orthodox Church, its original owners, and were to be installed in the iconostasis of the Orthodox Church of the Resurrection, Strachan Square, London, at a special ceremony this Easter. The priest in charge of the church, the Reverend Kallistos Bury, had said they were delighted by the kind donation on the part of the Turkish authorities, and he was sure it would do much to heal old wounds and improve Turkish-Greek relations in the future.

'A pretty piece of diplomacy,' said Cromwell.

'You could say that.'

'Theo's really rather good at that sort of thing,' said

Geoffrey, who had prised Oenone away from the bishop and dodged the canon to join them.

'How did you manage the hat-trick?' Cromwell pursued.

'You mean getting hold of the maesta?'

'Partly.'

'Vouniki, the Betterhouse Vouniki, had it from young Kostas.'

'Snatched from school.' Geoffrey contributed. 'The Vounikis were part of the firm redoing the electrics. I don't know whether they intended to kill the boy, but it happened. They've arrested poor Harry's cousin, I understand.'

'I have to admit I hated that bit. I know no evil of Harry himself. It seemed treacherous setting the police on. But then of course, there was the boy and,' he turned to Oenone, 'there was Ralph to consider. The police weren't eager to give him up?'

Oenone smiled her gratitude to Geoffrey. 'I shall always be in your debt.'

There was a pause. 'Poor kid, poor young Kostas,' Cromwell said.

'Yes, well,' Theodora took up the tale, 'Kostas's father was certain he wasn't going to have any more of his sons killed because, of course, the other twin, Peter, might have posed a threat to the Vounikis.'

'Why on earth didn't the Kostases go to the police?' Oenone asked.

'The police might have wanted to know how the Kostases came to be in possession of the maesta in the first place,' said Theodora.

'So they decamped to Cyprus for safety,' said Cromwell.

'No, actually,' said Theodora. 'He'd booked seats for both the boys and himself to go because he had plans to sell the maesta and it would have been more convenient to do that in Cyprus than in London. But when the maesta was stolen and his son killed, he didn't take up the seats.'

'Why didn't he sell it before?' Oenone inquired.

'I think they had plans to do just that. You remember the photograph of the maesta your uncle took with Dick Pound in 1974?'

Oenone nodded.

'I rather think that was part of the sales pitch which the Kostases, Jeremy Troutbeck and Dick Pound had in mind to make for the icon before the Turkish invasion rather clouded things.'

'So they put the scheme on ice,' Oenone relished the diction so untypical of her usual style. 'It would explain why Uncle Jeremy never spoke of it and why Dick Pound put himself to the trouble of getting the Kostases out of the island so swiftly.'

'How did the Vounikis become involved?' Barbara Brighouse had joined the group as a rest from being pleasant to parents.

'They'd already had a bust-up with the Kostases,' said her brother. Indeed Kostas père had had a go at one of the Vounikis with a knife and done six months for it. The Vounikis are a Cypriot family but, of course, Turkish not Greek. The word got round that the Kostases were looking for buyers and that the Greek government might be interested in purchasing so as to make some political capital out of this precious national art treasure, etc. So they thought they might as well put a spoke in that particular wheel and pay off old scores at the same time.'

'What I think is so clever of Theodora, 'said Oenone (Theodora forgave the patronage instantly), 'is your recognising a member of the London Vounikis in Cyprus when they all look alike to me.'

'And they're all so invisible too,' Theodora agreed. 'Actually it was the evening you dined with us at the Paradise Garden Betterhouse that I first made the attempt to try and separate them out. Of course I didn't realise then that Harry was a member of the Vouniki clan. In fact, I wasn't aware he was Turkish. My only impression was that everyone who served in the restaurant looked alike. I remember looking at Harry, Mr Vouniki, and then at the waiter, and then at the one behind the bar, trying to tell t'other from which. The only difference I could see was the tendency to grow a beard late in the evening on the part of the older pair. It was when I saw the barman on the plane to Cyprus and later in the Rotunda and later still amongst the Germans, I began to suspect there had to be a Paradise Garden involvement, whatever their nationality.'

'How come the Vounikis were willing to let Kallistos Bury have the icon?' Cromwell inquired.

'Well,' said Geoffrey and Theodora together, and then stopped. Dame Alicia hoved into view with Stella Stephanopoulos in tow.

'I was just saying we mustn't talk politics. But its quite difficult not to when most of the fathers in the room are involved in them at a very high level,' said the dame.

'Power,' said Cromwell, looking round the room. 'It's very unattractive.'

Dame Alicia chose to suppose he was being ironic. Of course, she knew and he knew that in the end the only things that matter in this world – and there is no other, she felt – are power, politics, money, influence or, failing that, at the very least, fame.

'It is so very good to have your distinguished husband with us, Mrs Stephanopoulos,' she said, turning to her guest. 'I see from *The Times* he's very much involved in the

Cyprus reunification talks. Let's hope something will come of it this time.'

'Nothing will,' said Stella. There was a harshness in her voice which made Dame Alicia's drawing-room clichés seem suddenly more than usually fatuous.

Stella swung round abruptly to face Theodora, 'I haven't thanked you properly yet for your help.'

Theodora sort to change the tone of things, 'I thought Jessica managed her double bass beautifully this evening in the *Stabat Mater*,' she said.

'Artistically she seems to be rather gifted, your young lady.' Her pastoral sense aroused, Geoffrey lent his hand.

Stella fixed him with a cold eye. 'I must join my husband and, I suppose, support him.' She turned from the group and started towards the tall military figure in Greek army uniform on the other side of the room. Dame Alicia felt she had graced their company sufficiently and waved to Admiral Topglass.

'Oh dear,' said Barbara. 'A rift. Have you met George Stephanopoulos?' she inquired of Theodora.

'No. Nor am I keen to in the light of his behaviour.'

'He connived at the kidnap?'

'He wanted the triptych reunited.'

'Not a silly wish,' said Cromwell.

'But not for religious or even aesthetic reasons,' replied Theodora, 'but simply to repair his own family's honour and for nationalistic politics.'

'Reunification of the island?'

'Reunification on Greek terms, with Greek domination and with the Stephanopouli as the instigators, to expunge a dubious and perhaps treacherous past on the part of his family, his father in the German war. The triptych from Ayia Maria in the Turkish half would have been a nice

symbol to bring Greek sentiment together in both main-
land Greece and Cyprus. Left to themselves the Cypriot
Greeks might tolerate power-sharing. If you stir up a bit
of national pride you can stop all that.'

'George had to get hold of the three icons then?'
Barbara asked.

'Right,' said Theodora. 'He knew his daughter had the
Virgin and child from her grandfather, and he reckoned
he could count on that one as safe for him. He knew from
the family's records that Lady Braithwaite had been sold
an annunciation by his grandfather in the twenties, and
that it had a provenance in Cyprus. Word had come via
the Greek network, particularly his driver Michel Kostas,
that the Kostas clan were getting ready to sell the maesta.
At first sight it all looked very possible. But he had several
problems. One, the Turks knew about the Kostas icon and
were intent on getting their hands on it. Two, Jessica was
keen on icons and had a religious appreciation of them.
She wasn't going to part with it for her father's shabby
purposes. Indeed she kept it locked usually, when she was
away from it, and the key in her own pocket. And three . . .'

'Three,' said Cromwell, 'the Braithwaite annunciation
had gone to the Bennet family. George discovered this by
accident when his daughter made a copy of it. So he
arranged a kidnap.'

'Of his own daughter?' Oenone was outraged.

'No. The intended victim was her friend Clarissa Bennet,
Clarissa was supposed to be taken by Michel Kostas's twin
brother, Dimitri. Only the description of the girl was inade-
quate. Both Clarissa and Jessica are fair-haired and they're
about the same height. Dimitri put his car where Michel
normally puts his, directly outside the school. Jessica piled
into his car, not having recognised it wasn't the embassy

one, and thinking he was his twin brother.'

Barbara Brighouse was forced to grin. 'Sounds Irish.'

'Certainly an absolute shambles,' Theodora agreed. 'It was a difficult moment for Dimitri when he passed his brother's car and saw his brother's face and his subsequent signals. Jessica says they communicated by CB radio, racing round south London trying to work out what to do. Neither of the Kostases was eager to return to George, a man with a nasty temper, and confess that they had kidnapped the wrong girl – his own daughter to boot.'

'Nasty moment,' said Cromwell, with relish.

'Enter Kallistos Bury,' said Geoffrey, entering into the spirit of the narrative.

Theodora nodded. 'He, in fact, was Jessica's idea. She said she'd no intention of giving up her icon to her father, or letting her father force her friend's family to do that either. The only person she trusted was Bury. He'd been kind, he was a priest, he'd taught her about icons. She rather took charge of the unfortunate Dimitri and steered him back to the Church of the Resurrection early the following day. Then she announced she was going to stay with Bury until, as she put it, her father saw reason. Meanwhile she told Kostas to tell her mother where she was.'

'Which he did not do,' said Barbara.

'No, instead, when he saw she wasn't going to go home, he did a bit of blackmail on his own account, and sent a letter to Stella hoping she'd collect the other two icons for them.'

'How did Bury feel about his unexpected guest?' Cromwell asked.

'When he heard the tales from Jessica, he decided he wasn't going to let the politicians have what he rightly felt belonged to the Greek Orthodox Church. So he entered the "reunite-the-triptych" game on his own account.

'Jessica, of course, was happy for him to have hers.'

'Right,' Theodora agreed. 'Then he consulted Mrs Bennet and asked her to sell.'

'Did she?' asked Oenone with curiosity.

'Not at that point. She did better than that in the end, however. When she heard he'd got the other two, she made a gift of her one.'

'Pretty good,' said Geoffrey approvingly.

'Yes. She said she was sure her grandmother's friend, Helena Braithwaite, would have wished it. Quite right, too,' Theodora added, thinking of her Uncle Hugh.

'And the maesta?' Cromwell pursued.

'This was Bury's great coup,' Theodora was admiring. 'He was really very enterprising. He got hold of the Turkish ambassador and suggested it would help Anglo-European-Turkish relations if (a) the icon was united with the other two by gift of the Turkish government, and (b) it wasn't allowed to get in to the Greek government's hands. Both reasons appealed to the Turks.'

'So why take it to Montevento?' Barbara asked.

'He didn't,' said Theodora. 'I told you. Vouniki – the barman – took it to Montevento. Or rather he took it to his cousin in Kyrenia. When the Turks decided it would be good publicity to let the Greek Orthodox Church have it, he was told to give it to the Greek papa at Montevento. Bury, however, didn't want that. It's much too vulnerable to being bagged both by the Turks or by Greek raiders. On the whole, give and take a bit, Strachan Square provides the best access and greatest security.'

'So what was in the parcel that Bury was carrying to the monastery?' Oenone asked.

'My turn,' said Cromwell. 'It was the copy of Lady

Helena's icon. The one done by Jessica. Presumably to show his bona fides to the Turks.'

'How did you know?' Geoffrey inquired.

'He asked me for it. Hours, in fact, before Stella Stephanopoulos did.'

'What a lot you all know,' said Oenone with distaste to Theodora.

'One thing I don't know,' Theodora admitted. She turned to Cromwell. 'Why did Clarissa Bennet faint in your lecture?'

Cromwell smiled. 'Could have been my *beaux yeux*. Or it could have been that she saw the slide of Jessica's Virgin and child which she knew was in Jessica's bedroom and assumed a closer connection between the two of us than is at all the case.'

'It's from mistakes like that,' Theodora said, remembering her discovery in Hetherington-Pollock's *Travels in Cyprus*, 'that art comes.'

EPILOGUE

Holy Terrors

The organ was improvising on the tune of *Hymns Ancient and Modern* number 270, 'Christ is risen, the terror now/ Can no more of death appal us.'

In the body of the church there was a respectable throng. Geoffrey and Theodora's people-visiting was beginning to pay off. It was felt amongst local people that the great festivals were to be supported whether one was of the same faith or none. A sprinkling of South West London lads inhabited the choir. Oenone and Ralph Troutbeck graced the front pew. A row of turbanned heads at the back betokened the Singhs, who had turned out as a family to inspect the results of their building skills. There wasn't a cement mixer in sight, only clean floors, smiling saints in their niches and above them a watertight roof. Most satisfactory, thought Mr Singh the elder.

In the vestry of St Sylvester, Canon Langthorne vested slowly. He was eighty-four and he had not been a quick man even in his prime. It was good of them to ask him back to celebrate the Easter mass for them in the newly restored church which his grandfather had built. Later, of course, they'd have to have the bishop down to do the official opening, but Geoffrey (what was his name?) had very civilly said he'd like him to do the Easter Sunday early one and breakfast with him and Gilbert Racy afterwards. Well, that would be very nice, to have a good breakfast after the rigours of Lent and Holy Week. Would it stretch to a grilled kidney, he wondered?

He looked at the vestments laid out for him on the table; all in the right order, he observed. Someone knew what they were doing. He took up the white alb and made his prayer. His vesting prayers were his own, drawn from the Armenian Orthodox rite. He was old enough to allow himself that latitude, he reckoned. 'Clothe me, O Lord, with the robe of incorruption . . .' When he'd done, he paused and looked round the vestry. It was not quite as he remembered it. There were, to be sure, sepia portrait photographs of the giants of the Oxford movements round the walls, with Thomas Henry Newcome in pride of place, framed in ebony. But the rest of the space seemed different. In one corner there was (Canon Langthorne had poked it to make sure) a cement mixer with a tarpaulin over it, and some sort of brazier, smelling (could it really be?) of curry. A storeroom, was it? Crates, wrapping paper and boxes all over the show. A boot sale, Geoffrey had said: the modern replacement for the church fête. A vase of white plastic daisies, presumably unsold, decorated the table of vestments.

He took up the stole and made his prayer. He hoped they'd got a properly trained altar boy. Something had been said about a Greek lad: Kostas, was it? Of course he had no objection to someone from a sister church helping out, and the Greek Orthodox Easter was another fortnight in the future. But he wasn't sure how far he trusted Geoffrey in the matter of training. He'd had to be firm when Geoffrey had offered his female deacon as server. 'If you have a woman in the sanctuary,' he'd said, 'then I very much regret I cannot celebrate for you.' He'd thought, but not actually said, that the deacon would do very well to serve breakfast later if she'd a mind to. Geoffrey had quite understood and didn't press the point. Theodora had said she'd be perfectly happy to grill a kidney for them all afterwards.

He took up the girdle. 'Thou shalt gird me with strength unto battle . . .' Well, life *was* a battle. Two world wars, countless lesser conflicts, the observed working of his own and others' hearts and passions over eighty-four years had left him in no doubt about that. It was a struggle against the terrors of the world, violence and despair within and without. We surround ourselves in our daily lives with images of outrage and evil and then wonder why we have no hope, no faith, no love. We need to arm ourselves with prayer and sacrament, ritual (properly conducted, of course) and artefact, something concrete for people to hang on to. What we need to do, he thought irritably, is to recreate a Christian culture.

He struggled stiffly into the chasuble. 'Let thy priests be clothed with righteousness and thy saints with joyfulness . . .' The bell – they had as yet but one – leaped into its last happy cadence and settled to the single G-sharp which signalled the beginning of the service. Well, it was Easter. He wouldn't see too many more of them, so let us celebrate the resurrection.

Geoffrey put his head round the door and gazed with awe at Canon Langthorne's biretta. Haven't seen one of those for some time, he thought. Theodora would like it

215

too, he reckoned. 'Everything all right?' he inquired.
'All Sir Garnett,' answered the Canon heartily.